DUCK SOUP FARM

W J Corbett

Duck Soup Farm

Illustrated by Tony Ross

MAMMOTH

First published in Great Britain 1992
by Methuen Children's Books Ltd
Published 1993 by Mammoth
an imprint of Reed Consumer Books Ltd
Michelin House, 81 Fulham Road, London SW3 6RB
and Auckland, Melbourne, Singapore and Toronto

ISBN 0 7497 1289 9

A CIP catalogue record for this title
is available from the British Library

Printed in Great Britain
by Cox & Wyman Ltd, Reading, Berkshire

Contents

1

Daisy Has a Great Idea

The sun was burning the mist from the surface of the pond when the children arrived. They wasted no time jumping aboard their home-made raft.

'Cast off,' shouted Chris Maypole.

'Aye, aye, sir,' cried Daisy, his sister, slipping the mooring rope from its stake. Pushing hard to give the craft a start, she leapt on deck in a flurry of arms and legs.

'Hoist sail, Mr Mate,' ordered Chris.

'Sail hoisted, Captain,' confirmed Dave Thomas, gazing up at the tablecloth drooping sullenly from the clothes-prop mast.

'Steady as she goes,' yelled Chris, grasping the table-leg rudder. 'Prepare to meet heavy seas, and keep a weather-eye open for dangerous reefs. And remember, try to mutiny and I'll clap the three of you in irons.'

'Aye, aye, sir,' chorused Daisy and Dave, as

they sat down and grasped their paddles . . .

The gang had been longing for this moment. At last they were casting off from the bank of the pond on board the raft they had painstakingly built over the past weekends. On this perfect morning, everything looked set to make this a memorable first day of their summer holidays. They weren't too alarmed

8

when the raft developed a heavy list to port; after all, rafts had personalities of their own. But when the list became a frightening wallow the fourth member of the crew defied Chris and mutinied.

He had been press-ganged aboard. He hated the sea and bullying captains as much as his collar. With the raft in danger of breaking up, Savage, Daisy's timid mongrel dog, stood whining in the bows, his bandaged paw upraised as if imploring the shore to come back. After two minutes of being a sea dog he was desperate to feel the good earth beneath his three good paws again. He was ignored.

'Are you two paddling in a straight line?' shouted Chris at the galley slaves in front of him. 'Why are we going around in circles?'

'It isn't our paddling, it's your stupid steering,' snapped Daisy over her shoulder. 'How can we paddle straight ahead when you keep swinging the rudder from side to side? Anyway, how can I paddle properly when I'm half underwater?'

'And I'm paddling fresh air,' complained Dave. 'My side of the raft is too high for my paddle to reach the water.'

'Probably because you didn't hoist the sail properly,' grumbled Chris. 'It should be flapping in a stiff breeze.'

'How can it flap when there isn't a puff of wind about?' Dave retorted. 'If you can conjure up a breeze, good luck . . . I'm not into miracles myself.'

Suddenly, they all realised that they were equally to blame for the voyage that was going nowhere.

They had a sail that wouldn't billow, a rudder that went crazy at the slightest touch, and all mounted on a raft built from rotting planks lashed to old car tyres. Their expectations had proved much too high. Boredom set in. No one spoke for a long time. Precious holiday minutes were idled away by tossing bits of rotting plank into the water and looking daggers at each other. Meanwhile, the raft drifted around in aimless circles. Savage was afraid and anxious, limping around the deck, whining and pining for the shore . . .

'Dog overboard!' yelled Dave, trying to cheer things up. He pretended to push the little mongrel over the side.

'Don't you dare! Not even in fun,' warned Daisy. 'You know Savage has a bad paw. He'd drown with the weight of those bandages and the splint round his leg.'

Savage howled his thanks. But his hopes

were still firmly set on an end to this swashbuckling nonsense. He just wanted to get ashore to track down a bone he had buried, though exactly where he couldn't remember . . .

'So much for the exciting first day of the holidays,' said Chris, bitterly. 'I wish I was back at school. I'll bet Captain Bligh had none of my problems before the mutineers tossed him into a rowing boat, of course.'

'So, what do we do now?' said Dave. He glanced at Daisy who was trying to entice a blue dragonfly aboard her finger. 'Come on, you're always the one with the bright ideas. What do we do now we can't go sailing?'

'As a matter of fact, I'm beginning to get a brilliant idea,' said Daisy, gazing thoughtfully at the flashing insect on her finger. As it flew away she raised her head and stared around. 'Have we ever really looked around our waste ground, at the potential of it? Just look and have a think . . .'

The patch of waste ground behind their cottages wasn't much to look at. Long ago it had been the village allotment where old men grew prize cabbages and leeks. Now it was a neglected field, growing wild grasses and thistles, buttercups and nettles. In and around

11

the field stood a few sheds that had once housed shovels and forks and trays of busily germinating tomato seeds. Now the sheds only still stood because they were clasped around by upwardly mobile brambles. At the bottom of the gently-sloping field was the large, bulrushed pond formed ages ago by run-off water from the surrounding high ground. From the pond a path wound upwards through the field to a farm gate that sagged drunkenly on its hinges. Beyond the gate was an overgrown wheel-

rutted track that snaked out of sight towards the village high street.

'Do you remember that programme on telly a few weeks ago?' Daisy went on. 'About those nice people who ran a hospital for hedgehogs found squashed on the roads? Even Dad had a tear in his eye as he watched it . . .'

'Which was very unusual,' admitted Chris, swatting at a dragonfly who was inspecting his spectacles. 'He usually only cries when he watches his Marx Brothers' videos. Then he cries buckets.'

'Crying with laughter is different,' said Daisy impatiently. 'Do you want to hear my idea or not? With all this spare land around us, why don't we open an animal sanctuary?'

'I don't think the hedgehog people would like that,' said Dave.

'No! No!' cried Daisy bouncing up and down in frustration. 'I mentioned hedgehogs as an example. I'm talking about pets who have to be boarded out while their owners go on holiday. Wouldn't owners enjoy their holidays more if they knew that their loved ones were eating proper meals and sleeping in comfortable beds, and being taken for walks and things? We could provide all that.'

'How much would we charge?' asked Chris, interested. 'How about one pound per pet, per day, that would be fair.'

'And two pounds per day for the difficult ones,' said Dave, their friend and neighbour, his eyes gleaming. 'I'm thinking about pet alligators. I've heard sinister rumours about snapping pet alligators in England.'

'No,' said Daisy. 'If we launched our project it wouldn't be to make money. Our clients would pay what they could afford on a voluntary basis. We'd only need to collect enough to cover our small expenses. Just look at all the lovely grub growing all over the waste ground. It's a perfect paradise for any animal.'

'For vegetarians, yes,' said Dave, gloomily. 'How about if you detest that kind of grub? Like me and my dad. Ever since Mum started going to her health classes and basket-weaving that's all we get . . . nuts cooked to look like steak.'

'Dave's right,' argued Chris. 'Pet dogs won't eat grass. We'd need lots of money to keep them in T-bone steaks and stuff.'

'And what if we were asked to board a chimp?' said Dave, ignoring Daisy rolling her eyes. 'How much would it cost to keep him in salted peanuts? And another thing, what if we were lucky enough to see an elephant lumbering up the track from the village? We could hardly keep him in tons of fresh buns on a donation plan.'

'Now you're being silly,' snapped Daisy. 'Only zoos and cranky people keep exotic pets in the middle of England.'

'Anyway,' said Dave, putting the damper on

15

Daisy's great idea. 'Who'd want to bring their pets to this dump?'

'We could soon whip the place into shape,' urged Daisy. 'For a start we could clear all the rubbish from this pond.'

'And the path through the field could do with weeding,' said Chris, beginning to fall in with his sister's idea. 'It'd be hard work, but that wouldn't kill us.'

'How about the old farm gate at the top of the path?' said Dave. 'That needs repairing and oiling to make it swing again. And the track to the village hasn't been used in years. We'd have to cut back the weeds and the overhanging branches so that the clients and their pets could walk up without being smacked in the head and stung to death by nettles. Daisy's idea is quite a good one but it's hardly practical. Where could we find the tools to make her project a reality?'

'From our fathers, of course,' said Daisy excitedly. 'They've both got sheds stuffed with spades and hoes and all the things we need.'

'And lots of tins half-full of paint,' agreed Chris.

'And all the old sheds could do with a lick of creosote,' said Dave, his enthusiasm mounting. Then gloom set in again. 'What father ever allowed anyone into his private shed? No father in the world would allow his precious bits and pieces to be plundered, just to spruce up a patch of old waste ground.'

'What if our waste ground had an attractive name?' persisted Daisy. 'That might make our fathers open up their sheds.'

'How about calling our project Animal Farm?' suggested Dave. 'It's the title of my dad's favourite book. He says I should read it, but I prefer Roald Dahl stories myself.'

'Foursome Farm, sounds nice,' mused Daisy. 'As there are four of us in on the plan, it sounds practical as opposed to silly.'

Savage, the fourth of the foursome, howled his defiance at being included in another of the children's dangerous projects, but his opinion was ignored as usual.

'Why don't we choose a name that will make our dads chuckle instead of frown?' Chris suggested. 'They'll be the fiercest enemies when we launch our project. How about Duck Soup Farm in honour of our dad's favourite Marx Brothers' film?'

'That's a stroke of genius, Chris,' whooped Daisy. 'For a brother you get brighter by the day.'

'I think my dad would go more for Penny Black Farm on account of his fanatical stamp-collecting,' said Dave, scotching the idea. 'I'm pretty sure he hates the Marx Brothers. And what if people brought along their pet duck to be cared for? The name Duck Soup Farm would suggest that we'd boil their pets in gravy as soon as they turned their backs.'

'You're wrong, Dave,' said Chris. 'People who love ducks are bound to have a sense of humour and realise that the name of our farm means no harm.'

'And don't worry about your dad, Dave,' said Daisy, dancing an excited jig. 'We'll soon bring him round when I think of another great

idea. In the meantime, let's get this sinking hulk to the shore. We have lots of work and thinking to do. And anyway, Savage is beginning to look distinctly queasy.'

The small black-and-white mongrel slithered across the deck of the raft to lick his mistress's sunburned nose, and offer his bandaged paw to be shook, which she fondly did. He was the first ashore as the raft nudged into the bank. Howling with relief he limped off to crouch in hiding in one of the old sheds. And there he stayed, certain that Daisy would track him down and apologise for taking him to sea, and also attend to his bandaged paw. In fact there was nothing wrong with the paw. Daisy was using Savage's body for first-aid practice before the tests she had to sit the following week. Savage whined and peered through a crack in the shed. Where was Daisy and why didn't she come? Sounds of splashing and shouting were coming from the direction of the pond. Swivelling his spying eye, Savage was glad to notice that his sailing days were over. All that remained of the hated raft was a heap of old car tyres and planks on the shore. Patiently, Savage waited for Daisy to hunt him down, to tell him that everything was all right. He was a long time waiting.

2

The Key Question

By early evening the children had weeded the path that wound up from the pond and through the wild field to the sagging gate. It had been back-breaking and palm-blistering work. This was because the tools they had needed were locked up in their fathers' sheds. Or, more correctly, in their 'shrines'.

'There's nothing more we can do without proper equipment,' said Chris, trying to swing on the rusty gate and failing. 'For a start we'll need hammers and nails and oil for these hinges.'

'Not to mention clippers and shovels to tidy the track to the village,' said Dave.

'Let's face it, no one is going to entrust their pets to Duck Soup Farm in the state it's in. We'll just have to confront our dads and explain our plan.'

'Explain our good cause, you mean,'

corrected Daisy. 'Duck Soup Farm is for the benefit of animals, not us.'

'Those old sheds are going to be a problem,' sighed Chris, wiping the sweat from his brow. 'We'll need something to hack back all those brambles. Then we'll need creosote and roofing tarpaulin to make the sheds fit for paying pets to live in. Dave's right, somehow or other we must part our fathers from the keys to their sheds. Though frankly, I'd sooner ask a Beefeater for the key to the crown jewels . . .'

And he wasn't joking.

On the door of Mr Maypole's shed was a sign that read: KEEP AWAY . . . DON'T EVEN RATTLE THE PADLOCK . . . AND THAT MEANS YOU. Daisy and Chris were well aware that the 'you' meant them. They had christened the shed 'Dad's Wendy House' because only he was allowed to play in it. Mr Maypole had smiled a grim smile when he heard their joke. But the door to his shed remained locked just the same.

Dave called his dad 'The Hobbit' because of his habit of going to earth in his shed when the ladies from the health club and basket-weaving classes came to call on Mrs Thomas. Dave believed that his dad felt more secure in his shed than anywhere else in the world. Which was why he never allowed anyone else in.

But in spite of all this jealous secrecy the children were familiar with every item in their fathers' sheds. They had spent a lot of time gazing through the dusty windows while the two men were at work. The tastes of Mr Maypole and Mr Thomas were disappointingly similar. Both of them hoarded near-empty paint tins and lengths of punctured garden

hoses. From the rafters of Mr Maypole's shed hung a model spitfire plane, on Mr Thomas's work bench a half-completed scale replica of a steam-engine. Boring, but typically, they both had a large poster of Marilyn Monroe on the wall. And of course there were tools in abundance, mostly unused.

'Isn't it unfair that the things we need belong to people who have Scrooge-type problems?' sighed Daisy.

'Think of all that paint going to waste,' said Chris, wistfully. 'Our dads will never use it, while it's just what we need for licking things up and painting a sign for our gate. It isn't fair.'

'Well, moaning will get us nowhere,' said Daisy, squaring her dungareed shoulders. 'We must put our cards on the table. We must make it forcibly clear that unless we get the keys to their sheds our Duck Soup Farm project will flounder before we've got it off the ground. They must both be home from work now, so let's go and tackle them.'

'Dad's having steak and onions for his dinner,' said Chris, brightening, 'so he'll be in a good mood. The best time to ask him is when he leans back in his chair and pats his belly, and says to Mum, "That was delicious, dear".'

'Another brilliant idea, Chris,' said Daisy,

beaming. 'What about your dad, Dave, what's he having for his dinner? Something to make him smile, we hope.'

'That's the trouble,' sighed Dave. 'Mum has put us on a vegetarian diet. It'll probably be bean sprouts and nuts shaped to look like chops and Dad will whisper dark threats under his breath.'

'You poor things,' sympathised Daisy. 'But there must be something that would cheer your dad up. Try to think.'

'Well,' said Dave, thinking. 'He's always happy when he's poring over his stamp collection in his private corner. That's when he chuckles and rubs his hands together and swears "the vow".'

'What vow?' asked Daisy, interested.

'The vow that one day "the little blighter" will fall into his hands,' said Dave. 'You see, he needs just one stamp to complete his triangular Chilean set. But for years "the little blighter" has refused to fall into his grasp.'

Daisy and Chris exchanged astonished glances.

'Well, would you believe it,' said Chris excitedly. 'We've got an Aunt Mabel who's always sending me stamps from around the world. She thinks I collect them, but I don't.

But guess what she mailed to me last month?'

'Only a packet of rare, triangular stamps from Chile,' shouted Daisy, stealing her brother's punchline. 'What if "the little blighter" is lurking amongst them? It could possibly be a certainty, or certainly a possibility.'

'A possible certainty that would make a nice present for your dad, Dave,' said Chris. 'Would that cheer him from his black mood?'

'He would float on air,' said Dave, cheering up himself. 'In exchange for "the little blighter" he would probably give us his Hobbit home and everything in it. But what if "the little blighter" isn't amongst Aunt Mabel's stamps?'

'Don't think negative thoughts, Dave,' chided Daisy. 'If we don't think positively, Duck Soup Farm will be a dead duck before it gets off the ground.'

'So, what's the plan?' said Chris to his jigging sister.

'Listen carefully,' said Daisy, 'for I'll say this only once. This gang will form a deputation. The meeting place, outside our kitchen door. Inside, our dad will be watching the six o'clock news on Mum's portable, and smiling as he mops up his steak and onion gravy with a bit of bread . . . he always does that. Then, just as

Bert Fish comes on the telly to tell us that there won't be any hurricanes, we'll stroll casually into the kitchen and wait our opportunity to tackle Dad. Then, when we've won him round to the idea of Duck Soup Farm and the key to his shed is safely in my pocket, we'll race round to Dave's kitchen door. When we stroll casually in, as like as not Mr Thomas will be hunched in his private corner over his stamps, his face all miserable because "the little blighter" isn't there. Is that right, Dave?'

'Maybe,' Dave agreed. 'Unless he's frowning over the instructions in his steam-engine kit.'

'Thinking positively, I'm certain that it will be his stamp album night, tonight,' said Daisy. 'So, Chris, when we troop into Dave's house, what do you do – after saying hello, of course?'

'I reach casually into my pocket and say, "Are these rare triangular stamps from Chile any use to you, Mr Thomas?"' grinned Chris, getting the idea. 'Then when Mr Thomas starts waltzing Mrs Thomas round the room, shouting, "I've got you, you little blighter," Dave takes over to demand the key to the Hobbit hole as payment.'

'Dave will not demand,' said Daisy, sharply. 'He will ask for the key politely.'

'Sounds great to us,' agreed Chris and Dave.

27

But Daisy was chewing the end of her plait, worried.

'Where is that dog of mine?' she puzzled. 'He's been missing for most of the day.'

The words were scarcely out of her mouth before a dismal howl came floating across the field.

'How can I have been so cruel,' cried Daisy. 'He must be terribly upset having his sailing trip cut short. He must be crouching somewhere, completely bewildered. Here, boy, here, Savage, come to Daisy!'

At the sound of her hail Savage dashed from his hide and raced across the field in joyous bounds, the wet and filthy bandage trailing from his paw. Panting and whining, he gazed

up to enjoy the sorrow in Daisy's eyes.

The ill-fated raft episode was already fading from their minds as the four set off through the swishing grass of the field. How would they win over two fathers whose minds seemed to be completely out of tune with a modern, adventurous spirit?

3

The Deputation

'Thank heaven I can smell steak and onions,' said a relieved Daisy, sitting up to the kitchen table. 'Well done, Mum, I knew you wouldn't let us down.'

'You will also smell fishfingers and chips,' said Mrs Maypole, raising her flushed face from her stove. 'Which is what you two are having. The steak and onions are for your father, who has to work to keep you two in T-shirts and trainers that never seem to last five minutes.'

'And Dad deserves his treats, Mum,' said Chris. 'I hope his steak and onions are the best he's ever tasted.'

'Then stop saying silly things,' said Mrs Maypole, heaping baked beans on to their plates and plonking their dinners before them. She wiped a wisp of grey-blonde hair from her eyes and glanced wearily down at Savage.

30

'Now what? You've scoffed a whole bowl of Meaty Chunks. Go and find the bone I lugged back from the butchers. That's if you can find the energy.'

'I think I can hear Dad's key in the front door,' shushed Daisy, folding a fishfinger inside a slice of bread and biting excitedly. 'I'll bet he can smell his steak and onions even through the letterbox.'

'And a bit later he'll be smiling his head off,' grinned Chris, happily. 'You really are a brilliant cook, Mum.'

With that the children scraped back their chairs and raced to the hall to greet their father, Savage in hot pursuit.

'All these years slaving over a hot stove, and

now I'm Mrs Beaton,' mused Mrs Maypole, greeting her eagerly-sniffing husband with a brushing kiss.

'I wish our kitchen smelled as nice as yours,' whispered Dave, wistfully. 'Ours always smells of air-freshener and herbs.'

'Be quiet,' hissed Daisy, raising her head to peer through the window. 'Bert Fish is coming on with the weather. Right, are we all ready? Do we all know what to do? And remember, think positively – and here we go.' With their courage fully bolstered the children entered the steamy kitchen.

'A king never ate better,' Mr Maypole was saying as the three hoisted themselves on to Mrs Maypole's draining board and eyed him in silence. He was mopping up the last dregs of gravy with a scrap of bread.

'Watch 'em, they're plotting something,' warned Mrs Maypole, plunging greasy dishes into her suddy sink. 'They've been acting peculiar all day. And how am I expected to wash up with this dog about to land on my draining board, trailing his disgusting bandage in my washing-up water? Why is my draining board always invaded when you lot want something?'

'Savage is up here with us because he's a member of our gang,' said Daisy, defiantly. 'Like us, he refuses to get down until Dad allows Duck Soup Farm to become a reality. So please don't nudge him with your elbow, Mum.'

'What "Duck Soup Farm"?' asked Mr Maypole, warily. 'It sounds like a Marx Brothers' film to me. But where does the "Farm" come in?'

'We chose the name because we knew you'd be pleased, Dad,' said Chris, excitedly.

'Pleased about what?' said Mr Maypole, frowning. 'I wish someone would talk sense around here.'

Daisy then told him everything. 'So you see, Dad, it's a sort of holiday camp for pets whose owners have been forced to go on holiday by their parents.'

'And we've already made a start on our project, Mr Maypole,' said Dave. 'We've cleared the rubbish from the pond, and we've weeded by hand the path through the field to the old gate.'

'As you can tell, Dad,' grimaced Chris, displaying his blistered palms.

'Now, what we desperately need is a lend of the key to your Wendy House – I mean shed,'

34

interrupted Daisy. 'We urgently need shovels and clippers and scraps of old paint to design an eye-catching sign to nail on the gate. Dad, in the words of your hero, Churchill Winston, "Give us the tools and we'll finish the job".'

'We promise not to touch your Spitfire,' vowed Chris. 'Even though you've glued the wings on back-to-front. We wouldn't dream of tearing them off and sticking them back on the right way round.'

'What do you know about building aircraft?' said Mr Maypole, annoyed. He pushed away Savage who had leapt from the draining board to offer a grubby bandaged paw in friendship. He glared at his wife. 'Are you in on this? What's been going on behind my back?'

'It's all news to me,' shrugged Mrs Maypole. 'I only cook and slave around here. But not for much longer if I keep having these ructions in my kitchen.' And out she stormed into her lounge to phone her friends in Weightwatchers.

'So, what do you think of our Duck Soup Farm idea, Dad?' asked Daisy timidly. 'We're really serious about it. This time we promise we won't get bored and start kicking balls through people's windows. You'll be pleased to know that we've started to grow up and act responsibly.'

'For a start the waste ground belongs to the council,' said Mr Maypole. 'I don't think they'll be too pleased to hear that you want to turn it into a zoo. And there are the other two cottages in the block. Have you thought what the neighbours might think about this hair-brained scheme?'

'My dad will be no problem, Mr Maypole,' said Dave quickly. 'Chris's Aunt Mabel has posted the perfect thing to make him see our point of view.'

'All the way from Chile,' said Chris, patting his pocket.

'As for Old Mac's cottage on our other side, it's practically empty anyway,' Daisy pointed out. 'When was the last time he poked his head outside his big glass porch? All Old Mac ever does is sit in his wicker-chair with the sun streaming in, reading the racing results and having swearing competitions with Scruffy, his parrot.'

'What Old Mac chooses to do is none of our business,' said her father, severely. 'After a hard life at sea stoking boilers, he's entitled to settle down in his cottage with Scruffy, to enjoy the last years of their lives. Just because he rarely comes out doesn't mean he doesn't exist. Always respect the privacy of others, young lady.'

'But what if Old Mac hates being private?' argued Daisy. 'He might be tickled pink to hear about my great idea.'

'So, will you help, Dad?' appealed Chris. 'All we need is a lend of the key to your tool shed.'

Mr Maypole leaned back in his chair and sipped his can of beer. For a long time he gazed at the anxious children ranged along the draining board, their eyes wide and hopeful. Then he smiled as if at some thought, perhaps some memory recalled from the days of his own childhood. His smile broadened.

'The steak and onions are beginning to

work,' hissed Daisy to the others. 'Look, he's reaching into the pocket where he keeps his keys. Remember, only think positive thoughts.'

'Very well, here it is,' said Mr Maypole, handing the precious object to Chris. 'But if Mr Thomas and Old Mac refuse to go along with your hair-brained scheme, then this key goes straight back in my pocket. Do you understand?'

'Yes, Dad,' said an impatient and triumphant Chris.

'Right, let's go,' shouted Daisy, jumping from the draining board. 'Thanks, Dad, we won't let you down, we promise. You'll be proud of us when Duck Soup Farm becomes a huge success.'

'Just remember not to treat my shed like you do your bedrooms,' said Mr Maypole, wondering whether he'd made the right decision. 'And Chris . . .'

'Yes, Dad,' said the boy, poised to dash out on the heels of the others.

'If you so much as glance at my Spitfire,' his father threatened. 'I've been building model planes for years, so never, ever tell me which way the wings are supposed to go on. Is that clear?'

'Yes, Dad,' grinned Chris. Then he was gone.

Mr Thomas was crouching over a small table in the corner of the lounge when the children and Savage trooped in. They were pleased to see that the table-top was strewn with scraps of bright paper and leather-bound albums. Mrs Thomas was sitting cross-legged on the carpet weaving a raffia basket, a vegetarian cookbook by her side. She peered short-sightedly through her thick spectacles and smiled as the deputation stood in a nervous row against a wall, as if waiting for the firing squad.

'Look, dear,' she said to her husband. 'David's brought his little friends for a visit. And oh, they've brought along a sweet old badger with an injured paw. Who said that the children of today are selfish hooligans?'

Savage whined and slunk into hiding amongst her finished baskets that cluttered up a corner of her lounge. He had noticed Mrs Thomas's yapping, snapping white poodle excitedly eyeing him, and he wanted no introductions.

'Hello, Mrs Thomas, Mr Thomas,' said Daisy and Chris politely. They glanced towards the man at the table who raised his head and grunted, his gaze immediately returning to his untidy table.

'Still looking for "the little blighter", Dad?'

said Dave with a nervous laugh. 'Wouldn't it be funny if it was under your nose all the time, or even in the pocket of someone right here in this room. That'd be a turn-up, eh, Dad?'

'A miracle, more like,' muttered Mr Thomas, not bothering to look up again. 'And to what do we owe the pleasure of your company?'

'Who'd like one of my home-made spinach fritters?' said Mrs Thomas, rising and pattering barefoot to her kitchen.

'Cheer up, Dad,' urged Dave. 'Miracles do happen sometimes.'

'So perform one,' said his father, raising his head and rubbing his eyes, and showing what a nice, kind smile he had when he wasn't frowning.

'Chris, Aunt Mabel's stamps,' hissed Daisy. Casually she said, 'We were wondering if these old stamps would be any use to you, Mr Thomas.'

'Sorry they're a bit crumpled, Mr Thomas,' Chris apologised, handing the man the cellophane packet on which all their hopes depended. 'We know you like stamps so we've brought you a few.'

Mr Thomas smiled his thanks. But his smile was cynical as he opened the packet and scattered the contents on his table-top. With bated breath the children watched as he picked up each stamp with his tweezers, only quickly to discard it. The hopes of his audience began to sink.

'Here we are, tuck in,' said Mrs Thomas, returning from her kitchen with a tray of spinach fritters and mugs of steaming mint tea. 'Oh, but I've quite forgotten the nice old badger with the injured paw. Perhaps he would like a spinach fritter?'

Savage yelped and buried deeper amongst the raffia baskets.

Just as the polite children felt obliged to cram another fritter down their throats, they were saved. Mr Thomas crashed back his chair, overturned his small table and spilled everything on to the floor. His left hand smote his brow, and his right hand was trembling as it flourished a tweezered scrap of triangular paper aloft.

'Be careful of the furniture, dear,' chided his wife. 'We don't want to frighten David's little friends away.'

'Angels, more like,' cried Mr Thomas. 'A miracle has just occurred in our lounge. Bear witness that out of the grubby pocket of a grubby boy has emerged the green, triangular, Chilean Discontinued, with the president's

head facing the wrong way. Do you know what this means?'

'I hope it means you've found "the little blighter", Dad,' whooped Dave.

'Absolutely no doubt,' shouted his father, beaming fit to bust. 'At last I can fill that ugly empty space in my album. At last I can close the page on Chile, and move on to the blanks in Outer Mongolia.'

'And Chris's Aunt Mabel is bound to visit Outer Mongolia as soon as Concorde bring their prices down,' said Daisy, delighted for him. 'Which means that she'll be sending him lots more triangular stamps, in all kinds of colours.'

'How can I thank young Christopher for his generous gift?' cried Mr Thomas, still smiting his brow. Then he dashed for the door. 'I know. It'll do us all a power of good.' And he vanished into the night in his roaring car.

Twenty minutes later the children, Savage and Mr Thomas were wolfing down fish and chips out of the newspaper, while Mrs Thomas padded around spraying air-freshener everywhere.

'Now then,' said Mr Thomas, burping happily. 'Is there anything else I can do for you children? Just name it. Come on, don't be shy, Christopher!'

'Actually, we were hoping for another miracle, Mr Thomas,' said Chris, hesitantly. 'Dave really needs to borrow the key to your shed.'

'For what?' said Mr Thomas, his eyes wary.

'For the creosote and the roll of tarpaulin inside,' said Daisy, quickly. 'As well as other bits and bobs. You see, Mr Thomas, I had this great idea about Duck Soup Farm and . . .' she explained rapidly.

'Mr Maypole has already lent us the key to his shed,' encouraged Dave. 'But we need yours as well so we can rummage for what we need.'

'And why not,' beamed Mr Thomas, tossing the precious key to his son. 'Feel free to rummage as much as you want. Just keep your hands off my engine, that's all I ask. I'm having trouble with the wheels, they only seem to spin backwards.'

'We won't even glance at it, promise,' shouted Dave, barging out of the house to catch up with the others. Savage beat them all, anxious to escape from the overpowering air-freshener and the yapping white poodle. In less than thirty seconds he had dived into Mrs Maypole's broom-cupboard where she threw her dirty linen in preparation for washing. While the children were excitedly conflabbing

44

outside, he was burrowing his nose into a pile of flowered sheets, trying to blot out his unwilling role as gang member number four in a fretful sleep . . .

4

Scruffy States His Terms

The children arose to the sound of blackbirds tuning their throats. Bolting down Weetabix and orange juice, they were soon turning keys in locks and rummaging for the things they needed, watched over by the lovely smile of Marilyn Monroe. Though dreading the day, Savage swallowed down his breakfast and limped to help them. A short while later the four were gathered outside Old Mac's back gate, armed with tools and purpose. Nosing over the top bar of the gate they could see the old man in his glasshouse, reading *The Racing Times* in the sun. Chris nudged Dave who nudged Daisy . . .

'Good morning, Old Mac,' she shouted down the path. 'We're the children from the neighbouring cottages. May we have a word about Duck Soup Farm?'

'Do you realise the price of oranges and

mixed nuts, these days?' answered a harsh voice. 'If I'd any sense I'd wring your neck and be done with it.'

The children looked at each other in bewilderment.

'But we've never cadged oranges and mixed nuts from you, Old Mac,' protested Daisy.

'Just look at the state of your filthy toenails,' the harsh voice scolded. 'It's about time I took my sharp scissors to them.'

Dismayed, Daisy glanced down at her open-toed sandals. Her pink, painted toenails didn't look all that bad.

'We agree about Daisy's toenails, Old Mac,' called Chris, disloyally. 'Her teacher also thinks they're a disgrace. She's been sent home twice because of them, even though her marks always make her top of the class. But, Old Mac, can we talk about something important? Like Duck Soup Farm, for instance?'

'Who needs cheering up then?' shouted the harsh voice, ignoring Chris. 'Let's sing a verse of our favourite song, eh?' And it launched into a calypso entitled, 'Yellow Bird, up high in banana tree . . .' in an unmelodious croak. It was just as well that the children knew the song and were able to sing obediently along. They were still singing lustily when the door of the glasshouse

swung open and Old Mac came limping up the path on his stick. He didn't look pleased.

'I won't have my Scruffy teased,' he said, gruffly. 'Get away from my gate unless you want to feel this stick across your backsides.'

'Are you saying that we've been arguing and singing with your famous parrot, Old Mac?' gasped Dave.

'We're sorry, but we thought it was you,' said Chris, amazed. 'If we'd known it was

Scruffy we wouldn't have answered back. Our gang loves dumb animals, especially the not so dumb ones like your Scruffy. I must say he's got a very nice croaking voice, Old Mac.'

'A beautiful singing voice, I think,' said Daisy, sincerely. 'He sounds just like our mum's favourite, Harry Belafonte, only a bit raspier.'

The old man smiled, but just a little. Then his wrinkled face frowned again. 'You still haven't told me why you're hanging round my gate. What are those tools for? I hope you're not planning a hooligan raid on an old man's cottage. I hear that's the hobby of cheeky kids these days.'

'Well, it certainly isn't our hobby, Old Mac,' blazed Daisy. 'We're here to get your permission for Duck Soup Farm. We intend to turn the waste ground into a home for pets who can't fly to Spain with their owners on holiday. We've got the go-ahead from our own cottages, now all we need is the green light from yours. I'll have you know that these tools are for heavy farm work, not for smashing the glass in your conservatory. And if you're worried about that prize marrow on the pile of horse manure, take it from me, this gang would never use it as a dartboard.'

Old Mac's eyes were twinkling now, but only a bit. 'Explain some more about this Duck Soup Farm of yours,' he said.

And the children did with much arm-waving, and digging and clipping actions.

'How do you intend to feed all these pets — that's if they turn up?' asked the shrewd old man.

'That's easy,' said Daisy. 'The waste ground is chock-a-block with grub. The pond is full of green weed and nourishing snaily things, and the field is choked with thistles and grass and clover. As for the more exotic pets, which we'll house in the sheds, we can always buy a few cans of pickled locusts and curried bats out of our donation money. And we can always provide tea and chocolate biscuits for the odd pet chimp. But in the main our guests will forage for themselves.'

'When I win the pools you'll have pineapples,' shrieked a voice from the cottage window. 'Until then, shut your beak or I'll stretch your neck.'

It was Scruffy strutting on his perch in full view, his dingy, mustard-coloured feathers fluffing angrily as he happily condemned himself to death.

'Scruffy worries about managing on our

old-age pension,' explained Old Mac, grinning. 'But let's make a bargain. I'll give you permission to use my part of waste ground on one condition. The condition is that you enrol my Scruffy as your first client.'

'But he's already got a home in your front window,' said Daisy, confused. 'He hardly qualifies as a short-term orphan.'

'He will if you agree to our terms,' chuckled Old Mac. 'You see, for years I've been meaning to treat myself to a few days' holiday at the races. If you agree to look after Scruffy until I come back, than I can go. So, what do you say to our offer?'

'Let's agree,' urged Chris. 'We can easily afford to put Scruffy up for a few days. Our mum has always got lots of oranges in her bowl, and Dave's mum must be snowed under with nuts, for her cutlets. As for Scruffy's holiday quarters, we can always shove him into one of the old sheds when we've done it up.'

'Oh, no,' said the old man, firmly. 'Scruffy likes a front window to look out of. And he likes to watch a lot of television.'

'In other words he insists on staying in a proper home,' said Daisy, chewing her plait as she pondered the problem. 'You and Scruffy certainly drive a hard bargain, Old Mac. Wait a moment while we consider it.'

The children and Savage went into a huddle. After a lot of whispering and whining they turned back to face the old man.

'We agree to your terms,' said Dave. 'Scruffy can spend alternate days in our front windows. And you can tell him that we've all got colour tellies.'

They shook hands all round, Savage included. 'I'll deliver Scruffy and his perch first thing in the morning,' said Old Mac, 'in plenty

52

of time to catch my train to Newmarket. By the way, whose doorstep do I leave him on?'

'Dave's for the first day,' said Chris, quickly. 'Just walk past number two and park him on the doorstep of number one with the herb patch in the garden.'

Dave looked pained but said nothing. Then, wishing them goodbye and good luck, Old Mac shuffled back down his path on his stick, chuckling every shuffle of the way. He seemed to be finding some secret thought highly amusing . . .

'Give me room,' cried Daisy, clasping a scythe very purposefully. 'Just watch these brambles fly. I'll clear this shed in no time.'

'I've got a better idea, Daisy,' said Dave, restraining her. 'As Chris and I have stronger muscles, we'll do the labouring work. It's your brain we need. Somebody has to compose the advert to put in the newsagent's window, and who better than you? Then there's the Duck Soup Farm sign that we need to nail to the gate. You're much more artistic than us.'

'I'm also as strong as you two,' retorted Daisy. 'How about that day in the park when I pulled that fat boxer dog off poor Savage? Left to you two, Savage would be lying buried in

our garden beside the budgies and the hamster.'

'That boxer dog was only rolling Savage over in fun,' scoffed Chris. 'Savage wasn't even nipped.'

'He just had lots of slobbering spit all over him,' agreed Dave. 'All dogs enjoy a bit of rough and tumble.'

Savage sided with Daisy. Whining in protest, he offered her his bandaged paw. Shaking it lovingly, Daisy murmured that it was about time she changed the dressing, but again her busy mind was ranging elsewhere.

'Oh, very well,' she sighed to the boys. 'I'll be the brains of the gang if you insist. You two

Tarzans can get on with the menial work. But remember, no slacking while I'm away. I expect to see the waste ground looking like a proper Duck Soup Farm when we meet again. So what are you waiting for? Let's have you stripped to the waist, getting stuck in.'

'We will as soon as you leave us in peace,' muttered Dave.

'I'll be off, then,' said Daisy. 'Come, Savage.' And away she raced, her blonde plait already ribbonless and streaming loose, with Savage close on her heels.

5

Duck Soup Farm Takes Shape

The sun was setting when the four met again. They gathered round the gate at the top of the field, marvelling and praising their achievements.

'It was hard graft, but we did it,' said Dave, proudly. 'The track from the village is now completely clear of weeds and overhanging branches.'

'I know,' grinned Daisy. 'I tiptoed past on my way back from the newsagent's. I would have offered you both a swig of my ice-cold coke, but I thought it might tempt you to stop work. And the sheds in the field look very posh with their lick of paint and tarpaulined roofs.'

'How about the gate you're swinging on?' asked Chris, glowing with pride. 'What do you think about the squeak that set our teeth on edge this morning?'

'What squeak?' said Daisy, pretending to be puzzled.

'Exactly,' grinned Chris. 'It's been oiled away.'

'It certainly glides like silk now,' agreed Daisy, perched on the top bar and swinging to and fro. 'Well done, you've both earned your blistered hands and bright-red sunburn. And if you stink of creosote, well, it's an honourable smell.'

'And so do you now,' said a gleeful Chris. 'We forgot to tell you that we creosoted the gate and it's still wet.'

Dismayed, Daisy jumped down from the gate and inspected the seat of her dungarees. Savage had been caught out, too, and his tail was now smelly and dripping.

'How about the advert?' asked Dave, impatiently. 'Did you put it in the newsagent's window?'

'Of course,' said Daisy. 'I typed it on Dad's typewriter in red capital letters to make it eye-catching. I can quote it by heart:

DO YOUR PETS HOWL OR MIAOW OR QUACK WHEN YOU PACK TO GO ON HOLIDAY? LET DUCK SOUP FARM GIVE THEM THE HOLIDAY OF THEIR LIVES WHILE YOU ENJOY YOURS. LEAVE YOUR PETS IN THE CARING HANDS OF DUCK SOUP FARM. WE DON'T CHARGE ENORMOUS PRICES, JUST DONATIONS GRATEFULLY RECEIVED. REMEMBER, DUCK SOUP FARM IS THE PLACE FOR YOUR PET IF YOU CAN'T TAKE IT TO SPAIN WITH YOU.

P.S. NO ALLIGATORS ALLOWED ON
ACCOUNT OF THEM FRIGHTENING THE
DUCKS.

SIGNED:
THE DUCK SOUP FARMERS

'Well, what do you think?' asked Daisy, eagerly. 'And the newsagent is only charging us ten pence a day. We'll soon get that back in donations.'

'You shouldn't have barred alligators,' argued Dave. 'That's discrimination. For exotic pets we should have simply charged a "danger down payment" to cover the cost of being sued if a duck went missing.'

'No, Dave,' said Daisy, firmly. 'There will be no alligators or profit motives on Duck Soup Farm.'

'We've got to be practical, Dais,' urged Chris, siding with Dave. 'What if we're lumbered with a pig who only eats truffles? Just one truffle would set us back weeks in pocket money. We should charge a fair rate for bed and board to cover the costs if things go wrong. We don't want to end up in the juvenile court before Mrs Protheroe for murder or starvation.'

'He's right,' said Dave.

But Daisy refused to listen to their argument,

which was only disguised greed for money. Instead, she triumphantly brandished two objects. One was an old Oxo tin wrapped in Christmas paper. On the front was painted the word DONATIONS. There was a slit in the top she'd stabbed with her father's screwdriver, just the right size for taking fifty-pence pieces. The other object was a square of hardboard. With a flourish she held it aloft for the boys to read. It was brilliantly designed with a frieze of birds and flowers painted around the border. At the centre in gold lettering was the legend:

DUCK SOUP FARM
THE PARADISE FOR PETS

'I never knew you were an artist, our Daisy,' said Chris, delighted. 'Let's get them nailed to the gate before the light fades. I've got a feeling we're going to be snowed under with customers in the morning.'

'I've got a feeling I'll be facing the music,' said Dave, gloomily. 'Old Mac has promised to leave Scruffy on his perch at our front door in the morning. What if my mum and dad refuse to take him in?'

'Don't worry, Dave,' comforted Daisy. 'Old Mac was probably pulling our legs. He was probably testing our determination to make a

go of Duck Soup Farm by throwing a jokey spanner in the works in the form of Scruffy. Do you really think that Old Mac wants to gallivant off to the races at his time of life? And even if he did, don't forget that we'll be saddled with Scruffy the day after your ordeal.'

'I wouldn't mind looking after Scruffy,' said Dave, biting his lip. 'It's Mum's Dinky I'm worried about. He likes to snooze in the front window all day. I don't think he'll take kindly to sharing his space with a raucous parrot.'

Impatiently Daisy changed the subject. 'But come on, you two, I want to hear the sound of busy hammers. The donation box and the sign won't fix themselves to the gate.'

To the sound of hammering, she strolled a short way down the track. As soon as the din had ceased she turned and strolled back, glancing casually at their work as she did.

'Perfect,' she cried, dancing a jig. 'If that doesn't attract customers, nothing will. Come on, let's call it a day. It's beefburgers and chips tonight, and I'm famished.'

Moments later, the grubby and sunburned children stumbled home across the field. As a rule Savage loved this time of the day. Slinking on the children's heels he would stop and listen through cocked ears for the 'thump' of a foolish rabbit out past its bedtime. But tonight, tripping over his trailing bandage with his creosoted tail beginning to sting, he felt too dejected to hunt rabbits. Once home, he went to ground in the broom-cupboard. Mrs Maypole had other plans. Holding her nose she dragged him out.

'No one eats until you're thoroughly scrubbed and changed, this dog included,' she snapped. 'And be warned, I'll be having a word with your father tonight. This Duck Soup nonsense is getting out of hand when you come back smelling my kitchen out. Daisy, take this

animal into the yard and attend to him.'

Chris went upstairs to take a bath and Daisy filled a watering-can with warm soapy water and gave Savage a good sprinkling. The stubborn creosote had refused to shift and was hardening so much that the dog could hardly wag his tail. All Daisy could do was snip at the matted hair.

Scolded and scrubbed, the three Maypoles crawled into their beds to dream about alligators and rabbits and swinging gates – but most of all about tomorrow.

6

Anthony the Second and a Green-spotted Cow

It was seven-thirty in the morning and already hot as the four gathered round the gate at the top of the field. The sign had dried out perfectly, its tempting message in bright colours almost blaring down the track that led to the village. Surely no child was silly enough to board their pets anywhere else than at Duck Soup Farm? Daisy and Chris were questioning Dave, who seemed to have the weight of the world on his shoulders. Just half an hour ago the boy had been almost bawled out of existence by his angry parents.

'Old Mac wasn't joking after all?' gasped Daisy. 'He dumped Scruffy and his perch on your doorstep and dashed off on his stick to catch his train. I thought you said you were getting up extra early, just in case they did turn up?'

'I overslept,' admitted Dave, shamefaced. 'It

was the argument and the singing that woke me up. I crept on to the landing and looked out of the window to see what was going on, but I'd guessed, anyway.'

'Your father was leaning from his bedroom window having a set-to with Scruffy below on his perch?' said Daisy, trying not to smile. 'Scruffy was demanding to know if your dad realised the price of oranges and mixed nuts?'

'And your dad bawled back that he didn't know the price of anything that early in the morning?' grinned Chris.

'Then Scruffy threatened to cut Dad's toenails with his sharp scissors,' nodded Dave, biting his lip again. 'But Dad really blew his top when Scruffy invited him to sing "Yellow Bird", that's when I knocked on Dad's door and explained about Old Mac and the bargain we'd struck.'

'He didn't forgive you immediately, of course,' said Chris. 'But at least your parents did the honourable thing and took Scruffy in.'

'I've still got to go home tonight to give a full explanation,' said Dave, miserably. 'Unless I run away and join the Foreign Legion, or something.'

'Don't do anything rash until tomorrow,' advised Daisy. 'If Chris and I also get it in the neck we'll join the Foreign Legion together. But enough of these petty worries. Doesn't Duck Soup Farm look beautiful? Just imagine, at this very moment the early-rising children of the village are reading our advert in the newsagent's.'

'Not only reading, but acting on it,' yelled Chris, pointing down the track. 'Here comes our first customer.'

Squinting into the morning sun, the four observed a small figure trudging up the track towards them. They were disappointed that there was no sign of a pet. A small boy, with a cigar box tucked under his arm, stopped short of the gate, planted his legs firmly astride and

stared at the sign, his lips silently spelling out the words:

'Duck Soup Farm. The Paradise for Pets.'

Then he glanced at the three children and Savage who were watching him intently. 'How do I know this isn't a con?' he said. 'Any crook can put an advert in a sweetshop window.'

'Our advert went in the newsagent's window,' corrected Daisy. 'And though Mr Jenkins sells sweets as well, it doesn't mean that he accepts adverts from any Tom, Dick or Harry. So, what can we do for you, small boy?'

'I'm not your "small boy",' was the annoyed reply. 'My name is Anthony Jenkins and I live in the sweetshop. That's how I get to read the adverts first. So why are you calling the old waste ground Duck Soup Farm? Anybody can tidy up a bit of waste ground with the right tools. But that doesn't mean they're qualified to look after valuable pets. Convince me why I should leave my pet in your charge.'

'As you haven't brought a pet, you can mind your own business,' snapped Chris. 'Go home and play with your plastic toys.'

'Who do you think you are, picking faults?' fumed Dave. 'Scoot back down the track, midget.'

'Who says I'm here to pick faults?' said the

boy. He peered in through the lower bar of the gate and received a long, wet lick from Savage. 'I must admit your advert told the truth. The old place does look a bit like a Duck Soup Farm. But talking about ducks, don't take in any alligators. You'll ruin the pond for ducks if you do.'

'Don't tell us what not to put in our pond,' said Daisy, sharply. 'Now, if you don't mind, will you please trot back to your sweetshop. I must warn you that Savage is a trained Duck Soup Farm guard dog. Our business is with people who have pets.'

'What do you think this is, then?' said the boy, tapping the cigar box. 'Tomorrow my dad is handing over his sweetshop to my uncle to run while we go for two weeks in the sun. The trouble is my uncle hates my pet, and the Blackpool landlady has refused to let him share my room. So I need to board him out where he'll be looked after and loved.'

'So you *are* a customer?' said Daisy, delighted. 'And our first one. Welcome, and we're glad you think Duck Soup Farm is the ideal home for your pet.'

'Meet Anthony the Second,' said the Jenkins boy, lifting the lid of the box. He fished around inside. All at once an orange and black tarantula spider scurried up his arm to stand eight-tiptoed on his shoulder, pulsing with menace. The Jenkins boy continued, 'But he'll let you call him Tony if you're kind to him.'

Savage howled, his front paws scrubbing frantically at his nose. Daisy felt very queasy as she forced herself to look at the horrible thing. Chris and Dave had backed nervously away.

'You can take Anthony the Second back to your sweetshop,' grimaced Chris. 'We don't board gruesome pets on Duck Soup Farm.'

'Gruesome?' said Anthony Jenkins, puzzled. 'He's my friend and I think he's beautiful. He'd only bite if you tried to squash him. What kind of Duck Soup Farm is this that won't take a perfectly nice spider? OK, I'll go and find a place that will really try to understand him.' He turned to leave.

'Oh no, you won't,' said Daisy, fighting her fear. 'If you love Tony, we will learn to love him too.'

'Where could we board him?' hissed Chris. 'We could hardly put a tarantula spider in the pond, or in one of the sheds.'

'That's right,' said Anthony Jenkins. 'Tony feels the cold nights a lot. He needs lots of warmth.'

'Where did he live in your sweetshop?' asked

Daisy. 'And what does he like to eat?'

'When the weather's cold he lives in Mum's microwave oven,' said Anthony. 'And to eat — he loves cockroaches and Mars bars.'

'Now, Daisy,' warned Chris, reading his sister's mind. 'Mum will go up the wall.'

'Anthony the Second can live in his box in a shed in the daytime,' said Daisy. 'But if the weatherman warns that the night will be cold we can always pop him in Mum's microwave, with the plug pulled out, of course. What could be cosier? She never uses it.'

'Anthony the Second will be pleased to be in such safe hands,' beamed the Jenkins boy.

'Now, about my complaint.'

'What complaint?' asked Chris, suspiciously.

'Your advert said nothing about offering free gifts,' said the boy. 'As a rule, new firms offer fantastic bribes to get their businesses off the ground. Like brand-new roller skates, and stuff. Now, my old roller skates . . .'

'On your toes, Jenkins,' warned Dave. 'Be satisfied that we've agreed to board your dangerous pet for a couple of weeks. But before you run for home, how about digging in the pockets of your shorts for a Duck Soup Farm donation? Don't pretend you haven't noticed the box on the gate. With your dad owning a sweetshop and newsagent's, you should be rolling in pocket money.'

But Anthony the First had been reared to be tight with money. Brushing his pet back into its hide, he placed the cigar box on the gate post and hared for home.

For some while the four gazed at it. The children felt ashamed. Within touching distance was Duck Soup Farm's first guest and they were too afraid to reach out and comfort him. Dave sidled forward and slipped a wine gum under Tony's lid, but even that seemed to emphasise their cowardice.

'Not getting at Tony, I wish our first

customer had been a woolly lamb,' sighed Daisy.

'How about a cow?' cried Chris. Instantly everyone was hanging on the gate, staring down the track.

'A cow without an owner?' questioned Dave. 'Who's ever heard of a cow answering an advert in a shop window? And why is it wobbling all over the place? Look, it's falling down.'

'And why is it white, and covered with green spots?' said Chris.

Savage leaned his dry nose on the lower bar of the gate and howled his frustration. Couldn't the rest of the gang recognise an impostor cow when they saw one? He sensed mischief, which could only mean more trouble for him. With his tail clipped to the bone, he had enough worries. He ran as fast as he could back to the security of Mrs Maypole's broom-cupboard, determined to stay there until Daisy's summer madness passed.

'It's a very brave cow,' said Daisy uncertainly. 'Look, it's struggling to get up.'

'It's the same cow that kept falling down and getting up in the pantomime, last Christmas. And we all remember who was inside that silly animal,' said Chris grimly.

'The Atkins?' gasped Daisy, angrily. 'Who are they trying to fool?'

'Us,' said Dave. 'Knowing those pushy Atkins they're a Trojan horse after a piece of the action.'

'Moo, moo,' appealed the cow as it wobbled up to the gate. It tried to nose its way inside but collapsed on its haunches as the gate was slammed shut. Moments later a head struggled free from the front half. As expected, it was Rosie Atkins, her angry face pouring sweat.

'Can't you take a joke?' she shouted. 'Anyway, you can't bar us from the waste ground. Me and Ben and lots of children from the village have always played here. Altering the name to Duck Soup Farm won't keep us out.'

'Why couldn't you have walked up the track like normal human beings then?' demanded Daisy. 'It's obvious that you're spies in that silly costume. Well, you can't come in. Unless you're customers, of course.'

'Which they're not,' said Chris, contemptuously eyeing the plastic cow lying crumpled on the ground. 'They can hardly claim that as a pet.'

'How about if we've come to ask for a job?' said Ben Atkins, folding up the cow.

'You're bound to have customer ducks on Duck Soup Farm and I'm a duck expert. I look after my granddad's ducks and geese all the time.'

'We've got no ducks or geese at the moment,' snapped Daisy. 'When they do come waddling in we'll look after them ourselves, thank you very much.'

'And who'll be looking after the pet spiders?' asked Rosie, smiling secretly. 'Our family went to the zoo once and the man in the peaked cap put a huge tarantula spider on my arm. It stalked up and down and I wasn't frightened a bit. The man said that I had a natural way with dangerous spiders.'

'So, you want a job, eh?' said Chris, casually. 'And you specialise in spiders? Anybody can claim that.'

'Don't accuse me of lying, Maypole,' warned tiny Rosie. 'Anyway, I wouldn't take the job unless Ben was employed as Duck Manager. As twins, if one gets a job the other must get one too.'

'Perhaps we can come to some arrangement,' said Daisy, quickly. 'As soon as the ducks come waddling in, Ben will be hired on the spot. But for now, Rosie, we'd like you to cast your expert eye at the gatepost. What do you think?'

'There's a tarantula spider in that box,' said Rosie, confidently. 'You can always tell when you've worked with dangerous spiders as long as I have.'

'Wait a bit,' protested Chris. 'How do you know what's inside the box without having a look? Do you know Anthony the First who lives at the newsagent's? Or have you been spying on us all morning? Even a professor of spiders couldn't look at a box and say what's inside it.'

'Open the box then,' said Rosie. 'Let's see if I don't know what I'm talking about. And who's this Anthony Jenkins the First you're going on about?'

'Who said his name was Jenkins?' triumphed Chris. 'You know more than you're letting on, Atkins. What if I said that the box on the gatepost was empty, or contained a grasshopper?'

'Then I'd issue a challenge,' said Rosie, looking him straight in the eye. 'I dare you to open the lid and put your fingers inside.'

'That's telling him, our Rosie,' grinned Ben. 'And if he gets his fingers bitten to the bone, it'll serve him right.'

Chris approached the box and lifted the lid a fraction, his hands trembling violently. Refusing to watch her brother humiliated further, Daisy rushed forward and clapped the box shut.

'You're right, Rosie,' she smiled. 'There is a tarantula spider inside. We were just testing you for the job.'

'Isn't he sweet?' cooed Rosie, plunging her hand into the box and allowing the hairy spider to clamber up her bare arm. As Tony climbed to explore her dark, bobbed hair, her face became serious. Coaxing him back to her forearm she announced that she was about to conduct an experiment that would determine whether Tony had a hidden, vicious streak in his soft body. Staring at him, she closed one brown eye in a solemn wink. The Duck Soup Farmers hanging over the gate were amazed to see Tony return her wink with five of his own.

'A tarantula spider always winks when he's happy,' explained Rosie. 'He obviously likes me very much and will only bite if we are parted. So, do I get the job?'

'And do I get one too?' demanded her twin, Ben. 'Don't try to duck me.'

'On behalf of Duck Soup Farm I enrol Rosie Atkins to take charge of our exotic pets,' said Daisy. 'As for our future ducks, they'll be turned over to Ben's capable hands.'

'We've got more staff than pets at the moment,' said Dave, gloomily. 'Rosie is the only member of staff with work to do.'

'And doesn't my Tony love bubblegum,' said Rosie, chucking the spider under where his chin could be. 'Now chew slowly, my darling, take your time.'

'Well, I haven't the time to stand around chatting,' said Ben, abruptly. He had been gazing down the track. In a swift movement he whipped a crumpled baseball cap from the back pocket of his jeans and clapped it on his head. It was a Donald Duck cap with a beak for a peak, and with large goo-goo eyes. A silly cap, but just right for a boy who lived and breathed ducks. His four eyes raised heavenwards in exasperation as Daisy suddenly cried:

'There's a duck coming up the track on a piece of string.'

'Someone is leading a duck on a piece of string up the track,' he corrected, adjusting his cap in a businesslike way. 'Don't talk about what you don't know. And of course you haven't noticed that the duck is panting and waddling like a drunken sailor? Do you know what that means? It means the duck is suffering from the deadly "duck gripe".'

'So the owner is probably bringing it in for a rest cure,' said Daisy, looking anxious. 'Will you be able to cope, Ben?'

'So long as you all stand back and mind your own business,' nodded Ben. 'My granddad taught me the modern methods of dealing with "duck gripe". In medieval days people didn't bother curing ducks. They just boiled them with carrots for their dinner. But we now know that on a strict diet of bread scraps and fresh weed, the illness disappears. The proof of the theory is a gentle squeezing of the belly. If the belly is firm there's no problem, if the belly is saggy, we've got problems. Now, if you'll stop talking me to death, I'll go and examine my patient.' So dismissing Daisy, he advanced to meet the duck and its owner, the beak on the peak of his cap nodding wisely.

In the meantime, Savage, who couldn't bear to stay away, was back and peering through the bottom bars of the gate. He had hated Anthony the Second on sight, but he quite liked ducks. It was then that he spied two more customers skittering up the track. Savage hated goats. His courage deserted him again and he raced off, howling for the safety of the broom-cupboard.

Chris and Dave were prepared to love anything if it helped to populate Duck Soup Farm. In a trice they had seized the leads of the goats from their owners and were enjoying trying to keep the clashing creatures apart. And then, suddenly, from one early-morning spider, the pets began to arrive at Duck Soup Farm and the donation box began to clink with coins.

It was the donkey who made Daisy's day. Around midday he came plodding up the track, all fat and grey, all sadly adorable. His name was Dob.

'You won't forget to show him his postcards from Spain,' implored the tearful girl, handing his halter to Daisy. 'Only he might think I've deserted him forever. Then he'll get all mournful and bray, night and day.'

'I'll do more than that,' promised Daisy, stroking Dob's tufty mane. 'I'll even read his postcards aloud to him. I suggest that you write on them, "Having an awful time, wish you were here". Choose dull postcards to send. If you can find some that show the rain in Spain falling mainly on your hotel, they'd be ideal to

keep Dob from braying in sadness, night and day. By the way, does he take sugar?'

'And parsnips,' nodded the grateful owner.

'Then get off and enjoy yourself,' said Daisy, cheerfully. 'And don't come home too sunburned or Dob will twig that his postcards were full of lies.'

By evening the six had time to stroll around Duck Soup Farm to check their charges were secure for the night. They peeped in the shed with THE AVIARY sign on the door. Inside, an assortment of birds were preparing for sleep with soft clucks and coos and cheeps. There were budgies in cages and pigeons in the rafters, and even a strutting magpie with a gold chain round his neck, his beady eyes intent on the glinting cross that hung around Daisy's neck. There was even an upside-down fruit bat who should have been a bird, but wasn't.

'I never realised I was a bird-lover,' said Dave, wonderingly. 'Yet I know them all by name already. I think I'm ready to cope with an eagle – if I'm lucky.'

In the shed next door the two goats and the black ram menaced each other from the end of their tethers, itching to butt seven bells out of anyone they could reach. In between bouts of temper they blissfully stuffed themselves with the lovely grub the children had provided.

'They'll soon settle down and become friends,' assured Chris. 'They only think they want to kill each other because they haven't got to know each other's personalities. A warm closeness will do the trick.'

THE EXOTICALLY DANGEROUS TROPICAL SPECIES shed was a disappointment. It was empty save for a lonely cigar box sitting on a high shelf that only Rosie dared to approach. Lifting the lid and winking inside, she returned satisfied.

'Tony is as happy as a lark,' she said, adding confidently, 'and we're bound to get some lizards and snakes flocking in tomorrow as company for him.'

'Is Tony warm enough?' asked Daisy, worried. 'Wouldn't he be more comfortable in our mum's microwave? What if the temperature plunges in the night? The weatherman's "hot, muggy nights" are sometimes frosty.'

'Nonsense,' scoffed Rosie. 'Tony is as hard as nails. He'll be frisky enough to leap at our throats for a welcome pat in the morning.'

The pond looked beautiful in the setting sun. On its orange surface floated four tame ducks plus three wild ones who had sneaked in illegally. Leaving the pond to walk through the lush field the children were pleased to see Dob nipping the tops off the thistles, his floppy ears drooping over his eyes. On an impulse Daisy reached out to give him a loving stroke.

The children parted at the gate, Rosie and Ben promising to be back early the next morning. Suddenly the Maypoles and Dave felt ravenously hungry. They had been working so hard all day that they had forgotten to go home to eat. They set off for the cottages that winked with welcoming kitchen lights, happy that their project was now a reality. Savage wasn't a bit happy. He was worried to death about his bald tail. He feared that it would never grow thick and luxuriant again. He whined and nudged Daisy's dungareed knee. Would she never come down from the clouds of Duck Soup Farm and understand the damage her obsession was doing to him?

As they neared the home cottages the children were alarmed to hear the sound of angry voices coming from the Maypole kitchen. Creeping to peer through the window, their hearts sank. A blistering row was in progress.

At one end of the kitchen stood Mr and Mrs Maypole, wagging their fingers and shouting. At the other end were Mr and Mrs Thomas,

their own fingers wagging, their own voices raised. The watching children quickly sized up the situation. The parents weren't at war with next door, but rather at war wth the centre of the kitchen. On Mrs Maypole's black and white tiles stood a tall perch with Scruffy on top singing 'Yellow Bird', in between beakfuls of Mrs Maypole's expensive peaches, quite unconcerned.

'Look at him tucking into my peaches,' raged Mrs Maypole. 'What right have you to bring him round here? He isn't ours, and never will be, thank heavens.'

'He's not ours,' shrilled Mrs Thomas. 'You complain about one peach? That bird emptied my fruit bowl within minutes of being in my lounge. And he's completely shattered Dinky's nerves with his bad language.'

'Shut up,' yelled Mr Maypole, trembling with rage. 'If you don't shut your trap I'll put my boot in it.'

'Don't you threaten my wife,' warned Mr Thomas, his fists clenched.

'I'm not threatening your wife, George,'

said a weary Mr Maypole. 'I'm threatening that bird. His singing is bringing on one of my splitting headaches.'

'And causing us to fall out for the first time ever,' said Mrs Maypole. 'We should be discussing this calmly.'

'And bringing those responsible to book,' agreed Mrs Thomas.

'You're both right,' said a grim-faced Mr Thomas. 'Where are they, anyway?'

'Outside, spying through the kitchen window,' said Mr Maypole, noticing three bobbing heads and one dry snout through the pane. He bawled at the top of his voice, 'OK, you lot, let's have you in here.'

Savage was the first of the four to obey. He came slinking in through the door and dashed for the broom-cupboard. Moments later the children trooped in, their heads bowed. In silence they hoisted themselves on to the draining board and waited for their severe ticking-off.

'We don't care what pact you made with Old Mac,' snapped Mr Maypole. 'All we care about is that you remove this bird from our lives, while we still have lives left. Is that clear?'

'Your father means it,' warned Mrs Maypole.

'So does Mr Thomas,' echoed Mrs Thomas.

'Very well,' sighed Chris, slipping down from his perch. 'We thought looking after Scruffy was a small price to pay to make Duck Soup Farm a success. But if you absolutely can't stand him, we'll just have to find him new lodgings.'

'Perhaps in a nice comfortable shed,' said Daisy, warily eyeing her father.

'Over my dead body,' snapped Mr Maypole.

'Scruffy and his perch would only take up a small corner,' appealed Dave to his father.

'Don't even dream about it,' threatened Mr Thomas. 'I'm grateful to you children for "the little blighter", but there are times when one needs to be ungrateful.'

'In that case we'll have to rearrange our plans,' sighed Daisy, jumping to the kitchen floor. 'Scruffy will just have to take pot-luck with Tony in the exotic shed. But I know that Scruffy won't be happy singing "Yellow Bird" to a silent cigar box.'

'Don't come the drama-queen with me, just get him out of here,' ordered Mr Maypole, pointing at Scruffy, who was squawking through every swearword he knew.

Savage slithered across the kitchen floor to

join them as the children set off across Duck Soup Farm to introduce Scruffy to his new quarters, and to his new friend, Tony. Setting the perch on the creaky floor, they saw that the bird was in no mood for introductions to anything. He was fast asleep, his head tucked under his stubby wing. On the shelf above, the cigar box remained equally mute.

Softly closing the rickety door behind them, the children filed back through the waist-high grass towards the lights of home. It was Chris who noticed the tall, stooping man, lurking around the gate at the top of the field.

'Probably just a trick of the moonlight,' said Dave, uneasily. 'Why should strange men be hanging around Duck Soup Farm at this time of night?'

'Besides,' said Daisy, trying to sound brave as they hurried for home. 'If there had been a stranger lurking round the gate, Savage would have growled and rushed to rip his trouser-leg.'

It was with relief that the children barged inside their separate kitchen doors, a terrified Savage beating them all to it. Soon the Duck Soup Farmers were hungrily tucking into their suppers while facing the music from their angry parents. But all good and bad things pass. Not much later they were tucked up in bed, dreaming about tomorrow and the adventures it would bring.

7

The Horse With No Name

Daisy rose sneakily early the next morning. Creeping along the landing, she deliberately failed to tap on Chris's door to awaken him. She felt the need to explore the magic of Duck Soup Farm quite alone. But Savage was a light and nervous sleeper. He came loping from the broom-cupboard to share Daisy's cornflakes in deliciously cold milk. His reward for his faithfulness was to have his bald tail pronounced fit, with a fuzz of new fur already growing. Savage's nose was much too dry, Daisy said in her first-aid voice. After smearing on some vaseline and capping it with a plaster, Daisy and her dog rushed out of the kitchen door and on to Duck Soup Farm amid a chorus of warbling blackbirds.

As they neared the sheds they were greeted by bedlam. The goats and the black ram had chewed through their tethers, broken out through the side of their shed, and were settling their grievances. Their battle wasn't two against one, or one against two, but each against each other. Bleating and charging, they remorselessly locked horns in their version of a medieval joust.

'Dash in and part them, Savage,' cried Daisy. But Savage had turned his cowardly back, and was pretending to count poppies in the field.

Meanwhile, from the pond came the sound of frantic quacking. The tame ducks and the illegal ones were voicing their distress at the sky where there hovered a duck-hawk, eyeing each duck for plumpness. Daisy was just about to run and throw stones at the killer when she heard the sound of music drifting from the patch of field where Dob nipped nettles. Her anger spilled over when Dob suddenly came lumbering through the grass, braying at the top of his lungs. Clinging to his fat back was Rosie Atkins, urging him into a gallop, her fingers clutching his thick mane as she sang, 'Yellow

bird . . . up high in banana tree . . .' in a very sweet voice. Seeing Daisy, she reined in Dob, looking more flushed than guilty, to Daisy's annoyance.

'We're supposed to be looking after our clients, not treating them like funfair rides,' Daisy shouted, jealously. 'Who gave you permission to come to Duck Soup Farm before anybody else was up? I invented Duck Soup Farm. I say who rides or does not ride Dob. Get down from his back at once.'

'I was only exercising him,' protested Rosie, sliding from Dob's back. 'And he seemed to enjoy it very much, so where's the harm?'

'Have you spared a thought for your real duties?' challenged Daisy. 'Or don't you care that Tony might be gasping for breakfast in his cigar box? And another thing, Rosie Atkins, who taught you "Yellow Bird . . ."? I'm beginning to think you're trying to take over Duck Soup Farm.'

'I'd never do that,' said Rosie, sincerely. 'I know that Duck Soup Farm was your great idea in the first place. I came early because I wanted to be useful. But Dob looked so lonely that I just had to give him a canter round the field. As for my duties, I attended to Tony ages ago. On my way home last night I called into Bob's Soggy Chip Café in the village. I asked Bob for a crisp-packetful of the cockroaches that infested his kitchen. He gave me all he'd got, or so he said then he begged me not to call the public health people. And those cockroaches were what Tony enjoyed for breakfast this morning, as well as a sip of my orange juice that Mum packed in my lunch box.'

'You haven't answered my second question,' said Daisy, a bit deflated. 'Where did you learn to sing "Yellow Bird"?'

'It was a parrot,' said Rosie. 'While I was looking after Tony this dirty-mustard parrot flew on to my shoulder and began to sing in my ear. Then he dipped into my lunch box and tucked into my orange and my peanut-butter-crunch that my mum packed for vitamins for me. Who is the parrot, anyway, Daisy?'

'Old Mac's Scruffy,' Daisy replied, feeling ashamed of herself. 'And I'd like to say I'm sorry, Rosie. I've misjudged you an awful lot.'

'Don't say sorry, let's just be good friends,' said Rosie. 'We all have Duck Soup Farm in our hearts. Why don't you take a spin around the field on Dob's back? He might be overweight but he sails over the smaller bushes like they were nothing.'

Daisy Maypole didn't need to be invited twice. She was soon cantering Dob around the field singing 'Yellow Bird' into his floppy ears.

Ordinarily, Savage would have been bounding along behind Dob and Daisy, but he was sitting on his haunches staring towards the gate at the top of the field, whining through his plastered nose and staring at a stranger by the gate. He began to bark and frantically chase his bald tail in circles.

'What's the matter, Savage?' snapped Daisy, interrupting her ride.

'He's barking at a man by the gate,' said Rosie, staring. 'A tall, bent-over man wearing a flat cap pulled over his eyes. Who can he be? He doesn't look like a customer.'

'It must be the man Chris swore he saw last night,' whispered Daisy, sliding from Dob's back.

Suddenly, the man hurried back down the track. It was all very curious, the nervous girls agreed. But then they were being hailed by two white rabbits sitting on the gate under the Duck Soup Farm sign. They raced to be of service.

'So you're off to cruise the Greek islands with your parents?' smiled Daisy, not at the rabbits but at a small boy who was resting them on the gate while he got his breath back. 'Well, you've found the perfect place. But wouldn't it have been easier to have brought them here in their hutch in your dad's car?'

'Indiana and Jones have never lived in a hutch,' scoffed the boy, wiping his runny nose

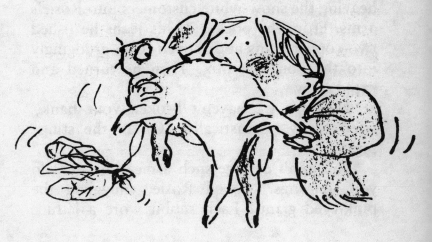

on Indiana. 'They're free-range rabbits. They live wild and free amongst my dad's cabbages and lettuces. Which is why my dad has gone all grumpy and refuses to allow them in the boot of his car. If you intend to imprison my pets in one of those broken-down sheds, you can forget it.'

'As if we would,' said Daisy, shocked. 'Indiana and Jones are welcome to hop as free as birds on this farm, and all for a small donation. They'll enjoy themselves so much that when you come back from the Greek islands they'll be twice as fat as they are now.'

'They'd better not be,' growled the boy. 'That would mean two journeys carrying them home. The same size but healthy, that'll do me and Indiana and Jones. Here, take 'em,' he said, heaving the snow-white customers into Rosie's arms. From the pocket of his jeans he fished two copper coins and shoved them grudgingly into the donation box. Then he turned and raced away.

'We hope we haven't broken your bank,' cried Daisy, sarcastically. 'Of all the stingy pigs!'

'You don't deserve such a mean master, do you, darlings?' cooed Rosie, snuggling the pink-eyed giants. Each rabbit wore a lettuce strung round its neck on a piece of string. They nibbled away quite unmoved by Rosie's love, and the fact that their mean master had deserted them.

'Well, we're not going to punish these two lovelies for the sins of their master,' declared Daisy. 'Whether that boy likes it or not, Indiana and Jones are going to enjoy their stay on Duck Soup Farm. What part of the field is free-ranging enough to make them twice as fat?'

'There's a lovely spot down by the pond,' said Rosie, her arms beginning to ache from the weight of her charges. 'It's overgrown with lush grass and buttercups and clover. I'll just go and settle them in before they tear my arms from their sockets. Won't be a tick.'

Two ticks after she returned, Chris and Dave came storming across the field from the cottages. A further two ticks after that, Ben came marching up the track from the village, his Donald Duck cap set at an aggressive angle. The three boys began to bawl out the girls and Savage.

'What's the idea, sneaking out before the rest of us?' they demanded. 'Duck Soup Farm belongs to the six of us, not just you three.'

Just then, Savage barked furiously. The

children stopped arguing to see what the fuss was about. Juddering up the track came a Land Rover with a horsebox bouncing behind. It stopped in front of the gate. Presently a man climbed from the driver's seat and approached. He was tall and stooped and wore a flat cap pulled down over his eyes. It was that man again.

'Can we help you, sir?' asked Dave, nervously.

'This Duck Soup Farm of yours,' began the man in a hoarse whisper. 'Is it a discreet farm?

Is it safe from prying eyes? Does it bed and board pets with no questions asked? Because I've got a horse. Well, not really a horse. Actually he's a pit-pony who looks like a horse. A tall pit-pony who's spent his life toiling down coal mines and wants to spend the rest of his days rolling over and over in very tall grass. Well, have I come to the right place?'

'You've come to the perfect place, sir,' said Chris, proudly. 'Our policy is to cater to our clients' every whim. If your pit-pony needs long grass and privacy, that's what he'll have. Some of our boarders are so private that they don't even know they're here, sir.'

'And your pet will be able to wallow in lovely fresh water, if he doesn't mind ducks and the odd alligator who might pop in, if we're lucky,' said Dave.

'But can you kids keep your mouths shut?' persisted the man, looking round suspiciously. 'If one word leaked out that this pit-pony was here . . .'

'He must be a very important pit-pony if he needs to hide away from the world,' said Daisy, awed. 'I'll bet he's very famous. I'll bet he's won lots of rosettes and medallions for hauling the most coal in his days down the mines.'

'You're perfectly right,' said the man in the

furtive cap. 'But the problem is, his cruel mine-owner wants him back to haul coal until he drops. Our poor pit-pony would be buried in darkness for the rest of his life if his master had his way.'

'Well, Mr Man, you can rest assured we'll fight that nasty master to the death,' said an angry Rosie.

'Wait a bit,' said Ben puzzled. 'I thought they banned ponies going down the mines years ago? Though I could be wrong, my speciality being ducks.'

'No, you're quite right, laddie,' said the man, quickly. 'But the evil mine-owner is determined to flout the law. He's vowed to track down his weak slave and force him back underground.'

'He'd be a foolish mine-owner to tackle the six of us,' shouted Chris, clenching his fists. 'We'll guard your harried pit-pony with our lives, and that's a promise.'

'Oh, and I see you have a donation box,' said the man. He rummaged in his coat pocket and pulled out a wad of banknotes. Peeling a few off he stuffed them into the box on the gate.

'Thank you very much, sir,' gasped Chris, his eyes bulging. 'We are honoured to welcome our new guest to Duck Soup Farm, no questions asked.'

'OK, Charlie, back him out,' rasped the man.

The six watched wide-eyed as a little fat man slipped from the passenger seat of the Land Rover and hurried to the back of the horsebox. After some swearing and clattering of hooves he reappeared, leading by the rein the most beautiful creature the children had ever seen outside show jumping on the BBC. He seemed to be all prancing legs and arching neck as the little man led him to the gate.

'I never realised that pit-ponies grew so tall,' breathed Daisy, falling totally in love at first sight. 'I thought they were more stunted like Dob. How did he ever get inside a coal mine with his head so high from the ground?'

'Ah, well, the mine he slaved in had a high roof,' explained the shifty man in the flat cap. 'Horses for courses, you see. The lower the roof the smaller the pony, the higher the roof – but you understand.'

'The mine-owner can understand one thing,' cried Rosie. 'This pit-pony can forget about the horrible old days in the dark. We'll give him happiness and light.'

'Are you going to take his rein then?' said the little man. He looped it over Rosie's gesticulating arm and waddled back to scowl through the window of the Land Rover. He

103

didn't seem much of an animal-lover. But perhaps his gruffness hid a kind heart.

'Now, remember,' warned the tall man. 'No one must know he's here. Especially the evil mine-owner. Me and my friend will be back to pick him up when the coast is clear. We plan to smuggle him abroad to a country that's got no coal mines.'

'Your instructions are perfectly clear, sir,' said Daisy. 'By the way, does he have a name? We like to be on personal, first-name terms on Duck Soup Farm.'

'Name?' muttered the tall man, glancing nervously round again. 'Who said he's got a name? I didn't mention a name.'

'In that case we'll call him Duck Soup after the farm,' said Daisy, happily.

'Just keep him under wraps, that's all,' warned the man, hurrying to climb into the cab of the Land Rover beside his fat friend. 'And if we find out that you've leaked our secret, we'll come and demand our donation back, get my meaning?'

'Just trust us, sir,' called Chris. 'We'll hide him in the longest grass, and mum's the word.'

The children waved goodbye as the Land Rover and the horsebox bounced back down the track.

'Just look at you, Duck Soup,' whispered Daisy, stroking their guest's nose. 'Aren't you the lovely one? You look just like Black Beauty.'

'Except that he was black all over,' said Rosie, staring curiously. 'Duck Soup has a white blaze on his nose. See, your stroking is revealing him in his true colours. Duck Soup has been dyed, and very badly, too.'

'It must be coal-dust,' said Daisy, inspecting her hand.

In the meantime, Savage was snuffling around Duck Soup's slim ankles. Quickly he backed away wrinkling his nose in disgust, the plaster on it now black as the grate. 'Duck Soup has also got four white ankles,' said Rosie. 'And it isn't dye, it's black boot-polish, I can smell it from here.'

'I knew there was something fishy about those men,' said Ben. 'I think this pit-pony is Champion the Wonder Horse.'

'Your imagination is as over the top as your cap, Ben. Champion died before we were born,' sighed Daisy. 'There's probably a very simple explanation for all this. Anyway it isn't our job to pry into why the men want Duck Soup to remain a secret. Our job is to look after him until they come back.'

'And they did give us a very generous donation,' agreed Dave. 'They might even give us a huge bonus if we mind our own business.'

'Those men did look very shifty though,' said Rosie, thoughtfully. 'Especially the tall one. I didn't like the way his eyes kept flicking all over the place under his flat cap.'

'Flat caps often make people look shifty,' scoffed Dave. 'I think we're making a fuss about nothing. Let's discuss how to spend the huge donation.'

'Let's stop distressing Duck Soup and lead him through the gate,' cried Daisy. 'While we're arguing the poor dear is gazing longingly at the green grass. He must have spotted Dob and is anxious to meet him.'

Swinging wide the gate she led their new charge inside Duck Soup Farm. Unbuckling his halter she gave him a loving pat on the rump. Whinnying with delight, Duck Soup kicked up his heels and galloped into the field to be swallowed up in the lush grasses.

8

The Last Customer

The children were fast finding out that running Duck Soup Farm and keeping their questioning parents happy required great skill. By the fifth day it seemed as if they were managing London Zoo in addition to sitting on stern, grown-up committees.

Savage fled for the broom-cupboard when the brightly-patterned snake slid out of the sack.

'Ah, a very dangerous coral snake,' said Rosie, expertly winding it round her arm. 'The secret of handling coral snakes is not to make any sudden movements. They can be extremely nasty if provoked.'

'If that's your attitude you can keep your Duck Soup Farm,' stormed Tracy, stuffing her pet back into the sack. 'I'll find somewhere else to board my Gertrude. I'll have you know she's the most gentle grass snake in the world. She's

never been anywhere near coral in her life.'

'I was only joking, Tracy,' said Rosie, blushing at her mistake. 'I knew Gertrude was a gentle grass snake all the time. It's just that we like to crack jokes on Duck Soup Farm. It gives the place a happy reputation.'

'Where will Gertrude live while I'm in Portugal?' asked Tracy stonily. 'I see you've got horses in that field. I don't want Gertrude stamped on.'

'Gertrude will be boarded with Tony and Scruffy, our special guests,' soothed Rosie, calming Tracy down. 'They're very gentle too.'

'I'll give your farm a two-week trial then,' said Tracy, tossing her mane of hair. 'If

Gertrude is smiling when I return I'll give a donation, in left-over Portuguese money, of course.' With that she flounced back down the track, her toes tip-tapping as she rehearsed a gypsy dance, pausing to pluck a dog-rose from the bushes and stick it in her hair.

The last-but-one guest to arrive was as troublesome as a barrelful of monkeys. Squealing and twisting like a slippery eel, it took all of Chris and Dave's strength to keep it under control. The lead around its neck was

useless. This particular pet only responded to its beloved owner. The boy watched contemptuously as, in desperation, Chris unlooped the belt from his jeans and buckled it around the pink pig's back leg.

'He eats two buckets of swill a day?' gasped Daisy as the boy issued his instructions. 'The greedy little pig.'

'Give him only one bucketful and he'll squeal your farm down,' the boy warned. Digging into his pocket he produced a handful of foreign coins to the gang's disgust and, moving as quickly and as twistingly as his pet, he vanished from view down the track.

'Let's get this noisy brute shoved in with the goats and that mad black ram. If he wants to join in the fight that's OK with me. I've had it up to here with the lot of 'em,' protested Dave.

'Perhaps they'll end up killing each other,' said Chris, trying to cheer his friend up as they dragged the squealing pig away. Ben watched them go, he and Donald Duck shaking their heads at the violence of it all. Then he wandered away down the path through the field to the pond to attend to his gentle ducks. These days he was counting more wild ones than tame. But Ben didn't mind.

The girls and Savage (who had returned)

dealt with the last customer. It arrived on a trolley inside a wire-netted cage. The two girls pulling the trolley insisted that the occupant of the cage was a true pet.

'You'll be prosecuted if the police find out about it,' warned Rosie.

'It's only a baby one,' said the defiant girls.

'Maybe, but an alligator is an alligator,' said Daisy holding up her hand like a traffic cop. 'And it's not coming on to Duck Soup Farm. Alligators like ponds and Ben would go spare if that thing slid into the water amongst his ducks. We're very sorry, but we have to draw the line somewhere.'

'Call yourself an animal farm?' scoffed the girls as they trundled their pet back down the track.

'Am I glad that particular pet has gone,' shuddered Rosie.

'And Savage has gone again,' said Daisy, despairingly. 'Back to his broom-cupboard, no doubt. He's such a little coward sometimes. The alligator could hardly have snapped him up, being behind bars. That's what comes of having an over-active imagination . . .'

With the shed mended and the feisty pink pig tethered inside with the goats and the black ram, the children could relax and take stock.

'The ducks are recovering nicely from the deadly gripe,' announced Ben arriving soaking wet from his duties. 'Even the wild ones. I gave them all a free medical check-up.'

'And Tony, Scruffy and Gertrude are getting on wonderfully together,' said a happy Rosie, joining them.

'Just look at Dob and Duck Soup,' breathed Daisy gazing towards the field. 'Don't they look beautiful outlined against the setting sun?'

'You can only see the tip of Dob's ears above the long grass,' Rosie pointed out. 'But you can see the whole of Duck Soup's head and neck. Yes, they do look very lovely together.'

'Duck Soup reminds me of that horse in the story who had wings on his heels,' said Daisy, dreamily. 'Just imagine if the story came true and he flew away in the night.'

'Very unlikely,' said Ben, ever practical. 'Duck

Soup will still be here as an extraordinary too tall pit-pony in the cold light of morning. And so will my ducks.'

Rosie giggled. 'We know another story, don't we, Daisy? About a you-know-what.'

'Just the kind of story Ben would appreciate,' said Daisy, laughing aloud. 'About a certain pet who was desperate for a swim in his pond.'

'Tell me, then,' said an irritated Ben. 'You haven't turned a pet away?'

'You can thank your lucky stars we did,' smiled the girls. 'We'll tell you the full story one day. Then you'll understand that we are duck-lovers, too.'

'Time for home, I think,' interrupted Chris. 'I don't know about you lot, but I'm famished.'

'When I came home from work tonight, what do you think I thought I saw?' said Mr Maypole, tucking into eggs, bacon, beans and sausage. 'I thought I saw a thoroughbred stallion galloping along the path through the field.'

'Really, Dad, your imagination,' grinned Daisy. She was perched on the draining board, a bread roll open in her hand as she waited for the sausage he could never quite manage. 'You must have seen Dob the donkey distorted by a trick of the light.'

'A donkey, eh,' mused Mr Maypole, tossing her half a sausage. 'So you're taking in donkeys now. I thought that this Duck Soup Farm was all about white mice and small creatures like that? I'm beginning to approve less and less. It's about time I investigated your goings-on, you two.'

'I've been saying that all along,' sighed Mrs Maypole, turning from her washing-up.

'Where's my half-sausage?' interrupted Chris. He was looking enviously at the grease trickling down Daisy's chin. He had an open bread roll too.

'So long as you remember where these luxuries come from,' said Mr Maypole, tossing him the other half of sausage. 'From my hard-earned salary, that's where.'

'We also serve who only stand and slave,' murmured Mrs Maypole. 'And will someone please stop that dog whining. It's going straight through me.'

'Savage, here, boy,' called Daisy slipping down from the draining board.

At the mention of his name the mongrel in the broom-cupboard pricked up his ears. But this time he didn't run straight to Daisy. She had ignored him too many times in the past few

days. He decided to sit the call out in stubborn silence. But after the third call his resistance broke. He raced to answer, the rotting plaster hanging from his nose. Daisy ripped it off.

'I think Savage may be going a bit deaf,' she said, inspecting his ears. 'He usually comes at my first call. He's probably got wax in his ears. What we need is some warm olive oil and some cotton wool.'

While the rest of the family went into the lounge to watch TV she attended to Savage's hearing problem. He stood obediently still while the girl stuffed cotton wool soaked in olive oil into his ears. At once he was plunged into a world of silence. There would be no listening to the cheerful dawn chorus for Savage the next morning. But he wouldn't miss that too much. At least Daisy was noticing him. And to gang member number six that was more important than all the whistling birds in the world.

9

The Dark Before the Dawn

The following morning was cloudy, with a spit
of rain in the air. For the first time the sun
wasn't shining down on Duck Soup Farm. But
it wasn't the gloomy weather that dampened
the spirits of the children. It was simply that
everything suddenly started to go wrong. It
became clear that many pets refused to live
off the land like in some story books. Many
of those on Duck Soup Farm demanded
supermarket food and made their point ear-
splittingly plain. It seemed that one of the
children was always dashing to the shops in the
village to fill plastic bags with nuts and fresh
peas and expensive fruit. Money was no
problem, thanks to the donation box, but it
was the constant dashing to and fro that was
wearing the children down. Especially
troublesome was when the wild and the tame
ducks on the pond stopped foraging for natural

food. To Ben's disgust and anger, someone had been feeding them expensive oven-baked brown bread with lots of fibre, and now his charges were turning up their beaks at anything else. Chris had his problems too.

I can't cope any more, he thought, his face as white as a sheet. The pink pig and the black ram have joined forces against the goats. If they break their tethers it'll be like the Charge of the Light Brigade all over again. As well as that I'm having to look after an assortment of white mice, hamsters and gerbils, and I've run out of cottage cheese and crackers again.

'Where's Dave?' cried Rosie, running from the Exotic Pets shed. 'I need to talk to him about Scruffy and what that wicked bird's done. Gertrude, who witnessed the dreadful deed, has curled into a bundle of tight coils and won't speak to me. I mean, I didn't do it, Scruffy did. So where's Dave? Scruffy lived in his window once, he should know why Scruffy has suddenly turned killer.'

'Dave has suddenly become an expert on rabbits,' said Chris sarcastically. 'He always manages to be down in the field by the pond when I'm sweating to keep the dangerous pets apart. That's when he isn't counting the money in the donation box.

'That's not fair,' protested Dave, approaching with a white rabbit under each arm. 'My work is just as dangerous as yours. I've had saucepans thrown at my head, raiding the village gardens to keep these two in cabbages and lettuces. And I've got rose-thorns in my knees to prove it.'

'Never mind about cabbages and lettuces,' wept Rosie. 'Tell me about the Scruffy you once knew. Explain to me why he's pecked one of Tony's legs clean off and is glaring at the remaining seven?'

'I can only guess that Scruffy is bored, and is missing his swearing contests with Old Mac,' said Dave, wearily. 'We can only pray that Old Mac comes home from the races as soon as possible.'

'My ducks are showing the signs of the deadly gripe again,' said a grim-faced Ben, toiling up from the pond and shaking himself dry like a dog. 'It's the special brown bread that caused it. I'd love to find out who's been feeding them without my permission.'

'And what's Daisy doing in the meantime?' cried Rosie. 'She's in the field with Dob and Duck Soup, that's where. It shouldn't take all morning to read Dob one gloomy postcard from Spain. Here she comes now. Just look, she couldn't wait to get on to Duck Soup's back.'

The four glared angrily towards the field. Out of the long grass galloped Duck Soup with Daisy clinging to his mane and singing 'Yellow Bird' at the top of her voice. Watching Duck Soup move it was plain that he had never been down a coal mine in his life. He was poetry in motion as he effortlessly leapt a shed, his white nose and ankles flashing. Rosie was just about to shout Daisy a piece of her mind when a hoarse voice hailed from the gate. It was that man again. The children and Savage trudged up to the gate to see what he wanted. By now convinced that he was a desperate crook, they hoped fervently that he wasn't hiding a machine-gun under his coat. They ignored Savage, who began to chase his tail in a terrified frenzy. He was almost deaf, so he wouldn't have come to heel anyway.

'Hello, again, sir,' said Chris, politely. 'Have you come to check up on your pit-pony? He's in the best of health, we assure you.'

The man ignored him. Pointing a bony finger towards the field, he snarled, 'Who gave that little brat permission to ride him? My orders were for him to be kept out of sight. How many other people know he's here? You promised me that mum was the word. I paid good money for your trust.'

'Only we five children and Savage know he's here, honest, sir,' said Dave, clutching the rabbits close to control his shaking.

'And you've also been grooming him without permission,' snapped the man. Then his voice became a confiding whisper. 'Didn't I make it clear that the wicked mine-owner was hot on his trail? He's looking for a pit-pony with a white nose and ankles. How can the poor creature remain incognito with his markings on display for all the world to see? Do you want him to be discovered and dragged back into slavery again?'

'We'd hate that, sir,' said Rosie, pretending she didn't know that the man was probably a wanted crook. 'In Duck Soup's interest we'll push Daisy off his back, paint his nose and ankles black again, then hide him in the longest grass we can find.'

'There's a good girl,' smiled the man. Then his voice filled with menace again. 'But just in case you forget, I'm taking a small precaution. Do you see that bush waving and thrashing just behind me?'

'Yes, sir,' whispered the frightened children.

'Well, hiding inside is my little fat friend,' warned the tall man. 'He's a pleasant chap as a rule. But when he's upset he flies into terrible rages, and runs amok with his pick-handle. What would upset him is if someone blew the whistle on his beloved pit-pony. For instance, if you children blabbed to some grown-up that the pit-pony was here, my little fat friend would burst from the bush with his pick-handle, and slaughter every animal on this Duck Soup Farm of yours. That's why he's determined to spend the night in his bush, watching and waiting for the whistle to be blown on a poor pit-pony who wouldn't survive going down the mine again. Do I make my meaning clear, nice children?'

'Your little fat friend would kill every pet in his frenzy?' said Ben, horrified. 'Even down to the last innocent duck?'

'If somebody blew the whistle, yes,' nodded the man, his eyes evil beneath his flat cap.

'You can tell your friend in the bush that he won't need his pick-handle,' said Rosie, trembling. 'If there's any whistle-blowing, it won't be from us. Tell your touchy friend to go home to bed with a mug of cocoa, he'll only get cramps in that bush.'

'I'm afraid he's determined to stay, just in case,' shrugged the man. Then he smiled a creepy smile. Reaching into his gangster-style coat he pulled out a thick wad of notes again. Peeling off a few fivers, he stuffed them into the donation box, saying, 'That's for lots of ice cream and crisps for some very understanding children. Oh, by the way, I'll be back with my horsebox tomorrow. We're moving the pit-pony on. I've contacted the Home for Escaped Pit-Ponies in France, who are eager to take him in. Just as well, that wicked mine-owner is too hot on the trail for comfort. Don't worry about my fat little friend in the bush with his pick-handle. He'll only leap out and go berserk if he hears the whistle blowing. Do you get that meaning too, charming children?'

'Every word, sir,' said Chris, faintly.

'Until tomorrow then,' said the man, loping off down the track. As soon as he was out of sight the five fled the gate and the waving bush, Savage howling in terror as he outstripped them all in his frantic haste to regain the safety of his broom-cupboard.

'What do you mean, I must stop exercising Duck Soup?' said Daisy, indignantly. 'Why is it a matter of life and death?'

When she heard about the man's veiled threats and about his little fat friend hiding in the bush, she was off Duck Soup's back like a shot. With shaking hands she led him deep into the field. There in the longest grass they could

find, the children tethered him, all the while casting nervous glances in the direction of the gate. Then they raced back to the safety of the cottage gardens.

'Now what do we do?' said Dave, chewing his lip. 'It's obvious that those men are crooks who'll stop at nothing if anyone gets in their way. Duck Soup must be a very important horse if they're prepared to batter animals and children to a pulp to keep his presence here a secret.'

'I've told you, he's Champion the Wonder Horse,' said Ben, impatiently. 'He's a bit like the Ugly Duckling who turned into a swan — except that Duck Soup has changed from a pit-pony into Champion the film star.'

'Shut up, Ben,' said an anxious Rosie. She turned to Daisy who was chewing the end of her plait and looking thoughtful. 'What do you think we should do, Daisy?'

'I think we should break our word to these men,' Daisy replied. 'We've got to do something we normally wouldn't dream of. Consult a grown-up.'

'I don't like the sound of that,' said Chris, dubiously. 'We've managed all right without them up till now. Anyway, they never help, they just fuss.'

'Be fair, Chris, grown-ups have their uses,' said Daisy. 'For a start, when they telephone the police they're always believed. If the little fat man should come charging from the bush with his pick-handle, grown-ups are the perfect people to phone for the Special Branch and back-up marksmen to call on the crooks to surrender when they're surrounded.'

'So which grown-up do we approach?' asked Dave. 'My mum and dad would just wave us away and tell us to stop being silly.'

'So would ours,' agreed Chris.

'Ours would just tell us to shush, and put us in hot baths,' sighed Rosie. 'Especially Ben who always smells like a duck-yard.'

'So without a grown-up my ducks are doomed,' said Ben sadly. 'There must be one grown-up in the world who would take us seriously.'

The words were hardly out of his mouth before a hobbling figure on a stick was spied just entering his garden gate. It was Old Mac home from the races, his pockets stuffed with the winnings he had squeezed from the bookies. Immediately, the children hared along the path to tap his wisdom before his gate clicked shut.

'I've never heard the like,' the old man chuckled. 'A pit-pony who jumps like a steeplechaser? A little fat gangster hiding in a bush with a pick-handle? And will you stop swinging on my gate, you'll bust the hinges.'

'But it's true, Old Mac,' pleaded Rosie. 'You should see Duck Soup gallop and jump. He cleared a shed with Daisy on his back as if it were nothing. A humble pit-pony could hardly do that, could he?'

'I've backed a few that tried,' grinned the old man. 'And most of 'em are still running.'

'Please be serious, Old Mac,' begged Daisy. 'Believe us in good faith. We took in your troublesome Scruffy, after all. And even though he's swearing as much as ever, Rosie sticks staunchly by him.'

'Even though he did bite a leg off Tony,' said Rosie, regretfully. 'And eyes the rest of them when he thinks I'm not looking.'

'OK,' said the old man, giving way. 'Let's see this gangster-filled bush of yours, but spare me the steeplechasing pit-pony, eh? Then afterwards I'll go home and enjoy my cup of tea with whisky then bed, if you'll allow me to. Come on then, let's get this wild-goose chase over and done with.' So saying, he began to hobble up the path towards the gate at the top of the field, the eager children helping him over the bumpy bits. At the gate they watched fearfully as Old Mac pushed into the waving bush, his stick thrashing. Moments later he returned looking peeved.

'Right, you've had your little joke on an old man,' he said wearily. 'Now if you don't mind I'm going home.'

'But the bush shouldn't be empty,' said Dave, astonished. 'See, it's still waving and thrashing.'

'Of course it is,' sighed Old Mac. 'All the bushes and trees are thrashing. You have

noticed that today is wet and windy? Or do you
kids think that every day is sunny and calm?'

'The bush may be empty but Duck Soup is
real, honest, Old Mac,' appealed Daisy,
clutching at his sleeve. But the old man shook
his white head and stomped off for home. He
had hardly limped a few paces before a head
appeared from a clump of thistles.

'Ah, that will be Duck Soup, the famous
steeplechaser,' he remarked dryly. 'And, I hope,
the last of your silly jokes.'

'That isn't Duck Soup, that's Dob,' shouted Rosie, clinging to his tapping stick. 'The real Duck Soup is staked out in the long grass at the bottom of the field. Please, come and see the proof for yourself.'

But Old Mac was having no more of it. Shuffling inside his gate, he clicked it shut behind him. Wagging a gnarled finger, he said, 'And I hope for your sakes that you haven't been playing jokes on my Scruffy. When you bring him back in the morning, I expect to hear him singing happily on his perch. And stop leaning all over my gate. It's not a climbing frame for you to bust.' And with that he tapped off down his path to prepare his whisky and tea.

'So much for asking a grown-up for help,' said Chris bitterly.

'Daisy came up with a rubbish idea this time,' agreed Dave.

'Other people have ideas,' said Rosie. 'Daisy is my best friend but my brain is just as good as hers.'

'Try and think of a way to stop my ducks being conked on the head,' said Ben. 'If you do I'll forgive you for cheating at Monopoly.'

'Shut up, I'm thinking,' snapped Rosie. The creases in her brow vanished behind her black fringe as she frowned and thought.

'And I'm thinking,' said Daisy, chewing her plait again. 'Much as I like and respect Rosie, my idea of how to solve our problems will be ten times as good as hers. This is it.'

The idea turned out to be one of Daisy's typical strokes of genius, easily as good as the one she had had on the raft, all those days ago. The children listened intently as she unfolded her plan. Savage had slunk from the broom-cupboard to join them again. Watching his mistress waving her arms and sometimes pointing at him, the dog came to the conclusion that another dangerous adventure was being hatched so he returned to the broom-cupboard where he was biffed on the head by a bundle of damp washing. He knew that Mrs Maypole hadn't meant it unkindly. He had already forgiven her as he snuggled amongst the T-shirts and jeans and tried to snatch some sleep. He had a feeling that his wits would need to be in tip-top shape in the morning. He had hardly closed his eyes, or so it seemed, when Daisy was clicking on the broom-cupboard light and leading him by one deaf ear into the kitchen. His heart sank when he saw what Daisy was holding in her other hand.

10

The Battle of Duck Soup Farm

'I knew this would come in useful one of these days,' said Daisy, holding up his detested tartan coat. 'It's chilly this early in the morning so you'll be needing it. Oh, but you probably can't hear me, can you? Let's have a look at those ears. They should be healed by now.'

The moment she removed the sticky cotton wool the sounds of the world rushed back into Savage's head. Or what little sound there was as the blackbirds were still tucked up in bed. Daisy's voice was a welcome loudspeaker in his head, even though she firmly insisted on buckling him into the despised Scotch contraption. After sharing the last of the cornflakes in cold milk, they crept out through the kitchen door. Ben and Rosie, wearing thick anoraks with the hoods pulled up, were leaning over the fence, impatiently snapping the heads off Mr Maypole's marigolds. They smiled with

relief to see Daisy and Savage. Ben had promising news.

'If the little fat man is hiding in any of the bushes by the gate, he must be sound asleep,' he hissed. 'Otherwise he would have rushed out and clonked me and Rosie over the head as we passed.'

'Well observed, Ben,' said Daisy, briskly pulling up the hood of her own anorak. 'Did you see any sign of Chris and Dave as you crossed the field? I know Chris is up and about, judging by the state of Mum's kitchen.'

'We heard them,' said Rosie, rolling her eyes. 'Their swearing was even bluer than Scruffy's.

Listen, here they come now.'

The muffled squeal of a pig rent the air. Then came the sound of skittering hooves and clashing horns. Above the chorus of squeals and baas and bleats could be heard the kind of coarse language that was usually heard outside Bob's Soggy Chip Café during school lunchtime. Only a little bit shocked, the girls stared to see through the cuckoo-spit mist. Suddenly a thrashing tableau appeared.

'What a performance!' gasped Chris, pouring with sweat. In one hand he gripped the trouser-belt that was attached to the squirming pig's back leg. To muffle the creature's squeals he had wanted to wind his England football

scarf around its nose, then thought it would not do much good. In his other hand he clutched a piece of rope that had been knotted many times in hasty repair. On the other end bucked a black ram with murder in his heart as he tried to get at the goats that Dave was desperately trying to control.

'Give me two tigers any day,' he fumed between lungfuls of air. 'My arms feel like they're dead, playing ring-a-ring-a-roses with this lot. And talking about the dead, I should think everyone in the cottages is awake by now.'

Daisy shot a nervous glance at her parents' bedroom window. Thankfully it remained dark.

'Right-ho, Chris,' she hissed. 'Hustle your charges into Dad's Wendy House, and make sure you tether them well apart. Dave, get those goats into the Hobbit hole. We can only pray that they'll all settle down and behave themselves. Now, Rosie, are you ready to do your stuff?'

'I run to the shed and collect Anthony the Second, and Scruffy and Gertrude,' whispered Rosie. 'Then, tiptoeing into your kitchen, I lock Scruffy and Gertrude in the broom-cupboard and pop Tony in the microwave that your mum never uses, though it sounds a lot of hard work, and I've only got one pair of arms. What will you be doing, or shouldn't I ask?'

'I'll be doing the most important and dangerous job,' said Daisy, hotly. 'My personal role will be to lead Dob and Duck Soup into Old Mac's glasshouse where they should be safe while we deal with the crooks. Savage will share the danger with me. He will stand outside the glasshouse and bark and snap like a fierce watchdog if the men spy Duck Soup and try to steal him.'

'And if you're wondering what my job is, I'm not telling you,' said Ben, secretly. 'All I can say is . . . at this moment the pond is completely duckless. While you lot were sleeping, I was studying a James Bond video. In the dead of the night I suddenly realised why he always won in the end. Because he always did the unexpected. Which is what I decided to do. If the little fat man comes gunning for my ducks with his pick-handle he'll be disappointed. For with a duck-calling quacker and a ball of string, every duck on the pond was spirited away to safety. And don't ask me where they are hiding, for even one of you could turn traitor if the crooks offered you enough money and jewels.'

'Thank you, Ben, you've made your point,'

interrupted Daisy, impatiently. She turned to the motley party of prancing, yelling animals and apprehensive children. 'OK,' she rapped, 'let's get cracking!' And off she dashed into the field. Savage, part-coward, but anxious for her respect, chased his tail a few times before bounding after her. Moments later the girl was stealthily untethering a nervous Duck Soup and leading him down Old Mac's path, shushing him to quieten his clattering. Once he was safely installed, back she raced to rouse Dob from his thistly-bed. She wouldn't stand for any braying nonsense, his safety was her sole concern. Meanwhile, the other Duck Soup Farmers were carrying out their tasks. At last, just as the sky began to lighten and the blackbirds began to sing, all was ready, the siege was prepared. Lying in the long grass and staring through their anoraked hoods towards the gate at the top of the field, the children heard the sound they had long feared. The sound of a motor chugging up the track . . .

'Oh, children,' called a hoarse voice. In the weak light the gang could just make out two figures. A tall, stooped one wearing a flat cap, plus the dreaded little fat man who appeared to be tapping the palm of his hand with the business end of a horrible pick-handle. The tall man called again. 'Oh, children, we've come for our pit-pony. Is there anybody here?'

'They're testing to see whether we're still in bed,' hissed Rosie. 'They're hoping that the coast is clear to force Duck Soup into their horsebox without us being any the wiser.'

'Well, we are wise,' said Daisy grimly. 'Let's just keep quiet and see what they do. Keep your heads ducked.'

'Just like the heads of my ducks,' said Ben, nodding his two heads contentedly. 'Mysteriously vanished, I'm glad to say. Now that they're off my mind I'm going to do a vanishing act myself. Quite soon. I'm going to crawl round the back of the crooks and let the air out of their tyres. Anybody who threatens to mess with my ducks, messes with me.'

'That's the spirit, Ben,' said Daisy, nudging him. 'If those crooks want a fight, they'll get one.'

'Where are they now?' said Chris, alarmed. 'I can't see them by the gate.'

'That's because they've just opened it and are creeping down the path,' said Rosie, eagle-eyed. 'Any time now they're going to find out that Duck Soup isn't there any more.'

'Which is when the fight will start,' said Dave, frightened, but determined.

Just as they thought, the sound of angry muttering was heard as the men discovered that their prize had fled. Moments later the tall man came storming from the field, his fat friend puffing along behind. The children were dismayed to note that they both wielded large, ugly lumps of wood. Then all at once the first rays of the sun illuminated the children, who were fleeing towards the cottage gardens.

'Hey, you lot, where's my property?' bellowed the tall man, reaching to grasp Chris by the scruff of his neck. With an agile wriggle, Chris broke free. Reaching the fences, the frightened children turned to face their pursuers. At that point the little fat man gave a triumphant cry and pointed with his pick-handle. The hearts of the trapped children sank. Though expecting to feel the pick-handles thudding on their anoraks, their concern at that moment was for Duck Soup. Why, oh why, had Old Mac decided to get up extra early that Saturday morning? The darkened glasshouse was ablaze with light. Clearly outlined was the old man gazing up in astonishment at the towering horse, then down at the plump frame of braying Dob.

'Brace yourself to stop them, Savage,' cried Daisy as the little fat man demolished Old

Mac's gate with a vicious kick. Roughly pushing aside the kicking and punching children the two men charged down the path looking very determined and ugly.

'Whoof, whoof, whoof,' warned Savage, baring his teeth as the men bore down on him. For once in his life he was refusing to flee when things got tough. He just managed to sink his teeth into the ankle of the tall man before being felled by a blow from the fat man's pick-handle. The brave dog slumped to the ground, a trickle of blood from a scalp wound staining his tartan coat. Meanwhile, Old Mac had realised the seriousness of the situation. Though afraid, his first thought was to comfort the rearing Duck Soup and the braying Dob. Patting their necks and muttering kind words, he could only watch helplessly as the crooks began to batter down his glasshouse door . . .

'Hang on, Old Mac,' Daisy yelled down the path. 'I'm going for help.' And off she raced.

'Mum, Dad, wake up,' she cried, hammering on her parents' bedroom door. 'Get on the phone to the chief constable and the parachute regiment. Duck Soup Farm is being taken by storm. Two desperate crooks are trying to re-kidnap Duck Soup, probably to turn him into French steaks. Please get up and throw yourselves into the fray. And, Mum, whatever you do, don't try to scramble eggs in your microwave. Also, if you need something from the broom-cupboard, don't poke your hand inside without switching on the light first. Please obey my instructions without question. This is a matter of great urgency.'

'The "urgency" is to give you a good spanking, young lady,' roared Mr Maypole, flinging open his bedroom door and glaring. 'Can't I enjoy my Saturday lie-in in peace, for once?'

'But you don't understand, Dad,' implored Daisy. 'Take a look out of your bedroom window and you'll see what I mean. Can't you hear the sound of breaking glass? But I can't stop, I must get back to the battle.' And away she raced. Arriving at Old Mac's gate, her worst fears were realised.

'Stand back, you brats,' the tall man snarled at the children. He stood guard at the gate while his fat accomplice led a whinnying Duck Soup out to the field. Behind was a scene of carnage. In the blazing light from the glasshouse the children could see the slivers of broken glass and the heaps of spilled soil and plants and broken pots. And amid it all lay Old Mac, Savage tenderly licking his bruised face and whining for him to rise.

'This calls for drastic measures, Dave,' shouted a grim-faced Chris. 'Let's go and get some fighting reinforcements. You know who I mean.'

Leaving Daisy and Rosie to harry the crooks, the boys made straight for their fathers' tool sheds. Unlocking the doors, they quickly armed themselves with two vicious goats, one surly

black ram, plus a pink pig with a squeal to shatter the eardrums of the most hardened criminals. This time the deadly four needed no dragging to their next destination. They were so angry at being disturbed yet again that all Chris and Dave needed to do was point them at the enemy and let them loose.

The men were hurrying Duck Soup up the path towards the gate when the Duck Soup Army struck. Urged on by Chris and Dave, the goats and the ram and the pig piled into the crooks, cheered on by Daisy and Rosie, who tore pales from Old Mac's fence and rushed to join in the mêlée. Then followed much butting and charging and squealing and kicking, plus some whacks on the head from Daisy and Rosie. Determined to hold out until Daisy's chief constable and the parachute regiment floated in from the sky to arrest the crooks, the children kept up their attack. They were rather disappointed when help arrived hurrying on foot through the grass of the field.

In the lead was a young police constable who had millions of years to serve before he became chief. Beside him scurried a lady constable with an earnest face and long eyelashes, plus a very pretty hat. Behind them came the Maypole and Thomas parents still in their nightclothes, their faces white with concern. In the excitement, only Rosie noticed that Mrs Maypole was wearing Anthony the Second on her nightdress as a very attractive brooch . . .

'Hello, hello, what have we here?' said the young constable, eyeing the crooks on the ground. 'Up to no good, I'll be bound.'

'Hello,' said the pretty lady constable to the children who were trying to catch their breath. 'I hope you are being good and behaving yourselves.'

Outraged, the children gasped out their story. They were not, stormed Daisy, juvenile delinquents who called out the police for a prank. And here were the captured crooks to prove it. Just then Old Mac came limping up wearing a large bruise on his head. Beside him bounded Savage, barking proudly as he showed Daisy his scalp wound and his rapidly closing eye.

'Constable,' shouted Old Mac, pointing at the shivering Duck Soup. 'Do you know who that is? He's none other than Gone With The Wind, the famous steeplechaser. He was kidnapped for ransom last week, it was in all the papers. And these two men are notorious villains who are always hanging around race meetings. The tall one in the cap is known as

"Slippery Sam". The little, violent one is known as "Fatty Bert". It's about time they were brought to justice.'

'So, are you coming quietly?' said the constable to the battered crooks on the ground. His eyes sparkled as he took out his notebook and pencil. This arrest could lead to rapid promotion.

'OK, you've got us bang to rights,' snarled Slippery Sam, now bald-headed as the goats munched on his cap.

'It's a fair cop, guv,' whined Fatty Bert, cringing as the black ram tried to charge him again.

They were quickly handcuffed and hustled into the back of a small panda car. Saying that he would be back to take important statements from everyone, the constable with his pretty partner drove back to the station, imagining the look in the sergeant's eye as the crooks were triumphantly locked in the cells.

'Excuse me, Mrs Maypole,' said Rosie, burning to ask the question. 'But do you know that Tony the tarantula is on your shoulder?'

'I know, isn't he sweet?' said Mrs Maypole, stroking him. 'I just couldn't leave him in my microwave when he kept winking at me. I think I must have a way with spiders.'

147

'Now everyone will know how gentle Tony is,' sighed Rosie. 'I only got the Duck Soup Farm job because everyone was afraid of him. I hope Daisy doesn't sack me for being a fraud.'

'Of course I won't,' said Daisy. 'But whatever happened to Ben? Where was he while the rest of us were fighting the crooks? I hope he didn't turn coward and run home because I like Ben very much.'

Her answer was a loud hissing noise that came from the direction of the gate at the top of the field. Presently Ben came marching towards them brandishing a large screwdriver from Mr Maypole's shed. He and his Donald Duck cap wore large smiles on their faces. 'That's stopped their gallop,' he said, satisfied. 'I've let down every tyre. If those crooks try to make a break for it with Duck Soup they'll find themselves as trapped as my ducks.'

'A very noble action, Ben, but I'm afraid the crooks have been locked up in the police station cells,' said Daisy.

'So you won't be needing my best screwdriver any more,' said Mr Maypole, snatching it back. Then he angrily addressed his children. 'I want a full explanation of all this, do you understand? I want to know how you got mixed up with crooks and never told me or your mother. Come, dear, let's go and use your microwave for the purpose it was intended. I think I need some scrambled eggs to soothe my nerves.'

'Here's sweet Tony back,' said Mrs Maypole, reluctantly parting with the furiously winking insect. 'And did you know he's got a leg missing?' Then she turned and followed her husband back to their cottage.

'How about my Scruffy?' demanded Old Mac. 'I think I'd better take him home now, before he gets caught up in more of your dangerous adventures.'

'Just follow our mum and dad and look in

our broom-cupboard,' advised Chris as the old man stomped unsteadily off on his stick.

'By the way, Ben,' said Dave, interested. 'Where did you hide your ducks?'

'In your outside loo,' grinned Ben. 'The crooks would never have thought of looking there. It was simple really. If you have a long enough piece of string and can make realistic quacking noises, ducks will follow you anywhere.'

Clutching at her heart, Mrs Thomas hurried away on her husband's arm to shoo Ben's charges from her spick-and-spotless outside lavatory.

The four parents came round very quickly the next day. It seemed that everyone in the three cottages was in the Sunday newspapers. Suddenly they were famous. The article the gang liked best was the one that started:

BRAVE CHILDREN AND DOG FOIL
RACEHORSE KIDNAPPERS. RUMOURED THAT
THEY ARE TO RECEIVE MEDALS FROM THE
QUEEN. WILL IT BE NEXT STOP BUCKINGHAM
PALACE FOR THE SIX WHO CALL
THEMSELVES 'JUST SIMPLE DUCK SOUP
FARMERS'?

After waiting some days for the royal telegrams to arrive, the excited children began to realise that the Queen probably didn't read that particular Sunday paper. But they were pleased to be paid a special visit by nice Mr Wilks. Mr Wilks wore a trilby hat and binoculars round his neck. He was the owner of Duck Soup, or rather, 'Gone With The Wind'.

In a small ceremony by the gate at the top of the field, Mr Wilks presented the children and Savage with a large silver cup, inscribed:

PRESENTED TO THE DUCK SOUP FARM SIX
FOR EXTREME BRAVERY

A proud Daisy announced that they would mount it on the gate to impress future customers. And also to attract larger sums of money into the donation box, said a canny Chris.

Then Mr Wilks said that he would like to give them a small, personal reward each, and what would they like?

'As my reward I'd like to go on safari with Sir David Attenborough to the most spidery jungle in the world,' said Rosie dreamily.

'I'd like an electronic "duck counter" with lots of winking lights,' said Ben. 'Counting

ducks by hand is a wet business when you fall in the pond.'

Chris and Dave agreed that for their reward they wouldn't turn down a large sum of money each in cash, while Daisy – well, Daisy was certain what she wanted.

'I want to ride Gone With The Wind in the Grand National,' she said, emphatically. 'And when he's leaping the fences ahead of all the others, I'll whisper in his ear, "Well done, Duck Soup, for you'll always be Duck Soup to me."'

Mr Wilks was very nice about it. He said that though he sympathised with their hopes and dreams, would they settle for a day out at the zoo with all the trimmings? The children did and enjoyed it very much. A very nice man, Mr Wilks, a very nice man indeed.

After all the fuss had died down a small boy came marching up the track from the village. He looked very suntanned and healthy. It was Anthony Jenkins from the sweetshop, come to take Anthony the Second home. The six watched silently as Rosie handed over the cigar box. They were digging their nails into their palms as the boy opened the lid to examine his pet.

'He's got a leg missing,' he said accusingly. 'What's happened to Tony's leg?'

'Why don't you examine the top of the lid,' said Rosie, her fingers crossed behind her back.

The boy closed the box and looked. Pasted to the top was a cardboard medal bearing gold-painted letters that read:

PRESENTED TO ANTHONY THE SECOND
WHO HEROICALLY LOST A LEG DURING THE
BATTLE OF DUCK SOUP FARM. IN LOVING
MEMORY OF HIS LOST LIMB. WE SALUTE HIM.

'My Tony, a hero?' said the Jenkins boy, pride in his eyes. 'But I always knew he was special. And he's got plenty of legs left, anyway.' And he marched back to the sweetshop, bearing the cigar box before him like some precious relic.

'Well, that little show got us off the hook,' said Ben, shaking his head. 'Myself, I prefer good old-fashioned honesty. Tony lost his leg because Scruffy is a mean, vicious parrot. But be that as it may, if you lot want to tell lies, I'll go back to my pond and talk honestly with good honest ducks.' And he did.

Savage was whining and pawing at his neck, and gazing up at Daisy through his good eye. He was trying to point out that he also had a medal for bravery hanging around his neck. Daisy patted him. 'We know, Savage, you're just as much a hero as anyone. And remind me to get a bit of steak for that eye of yours. Or would you rather have it in your bowl with a nice drop of gravy?'

'Hello,' said Chris, looking down the track. 'There're two girls heading our way, and dragging a wire-netted cage on a trolley.'

'What pet needs to be wired in?' said Dave, interested.

Rosie and Daisy knew. They sighed. The owners of the alligator were making a second bid to win bed and board for their pet. They had obviously been turned away from everywhere else, and were throwing themselves on the mercy of Duck Soup Farm again.

'Well, whatever's inside that wire-netting, Duck Soup Farm never turns a pet away,' said Chris. 'I'll open the gate and welcome them.'

Ben was down at the pond fussing over his ducks. Though soaked, he was blissfully content. It was just as well that he couldn't hear the argument raging round the gate at the top of the field. The last thing he needed in his pond was a snapping alligator who would seriously disturb his ducks. But for the moment, he could enjoy his peace and quiet. Duck Soup Farm was that kind of place – usually. The kind of place where the sun shone, where the clouds never blackened the horizon and adventures began . . .

Also by W J Corbett

DEAR GRUMBLE

When Tom and Clare Price hear the sound of
hooves clip-clopping up the lane and the familiar
cry of 'Any old rags?' they are ready to swap their
old woollens for the rag-and-bone man's goldfish.
But then they see something 'a little larger' tied to
the back of the cart – something so special that
spoilt Felicity wants it too . . . The race is on . . .

'. . . full of delightful eccentricities and jokes – the
manner is sublime.'

Robert Westall

W J Corbett

LITTLE ELEPHANT

Tumf (short for Tumffington) is the luckiest little elephant in Africa until the terrible day when the ivory poachers make him an orphan.

Tumf sets out on a nightmarish journey but finds friends along the way, including a veagle (a vulture posing as an eagle?), a tortoise and a cheeky little monkey.

Across Africa, through desert and swamp, water and land, happy and sad, Tumf plods on in his quest for happiness.

A funny and touching story by the author of *The Song of Pentecost*, winner of the Whitbread Award.

'The author has a great capacity for endowing his creations with the fancies and foibles we humans recognise as our own. His animals seem to behave just that bit more responsibly . . .'

The Junior Bookshelf

A selected list of titles available from Mammoth

While every effort is made to keep prices low, it is sometimes necessary to increase prices at short notice. Mandarin Paperbacks reserves the right to show new retail prices on covers which may differ from those previously advertised in the text or elsewhere.

The prices shown below were correct at the time of going to press.

☐	7497 0366 0	**Dilly the Dinosaur**	Tony Bradman	£2.50
☐	7497 0137 4	**Flat Stanley**	Jeff Brown	£2.50
☐	7497 0306 7	**The Chocolate Touch**	P Skene Catling	£2.50
☐	7497 0568 X	**Dorrie and the Goblin**	Patricia Coombs	£2.50
☐	7497 0114 5	**Dear Grumble**	W J Corbett	£2.50
☐	7497 0054 8	**My Naughty Little Sister**	Dorothy Edwards	£2.50
☐	7497 0723 2	**The Little Prince (colour ed.)**	A Saint-Exupery	£3.99
☐	7497 0305 9	**Bill's New Frock**	Anne Fine	£2.99
☐	7497 0590 6	**Wild Robert**	Diana Wynne Jones	£2.50
☐	7497 0661 9	**The Six Bullerby Children**	Astrid Lindgren	£2.50
☐	7497 0319 9	**Dr Monsoon Taggert's Amazing Finishing Academy**	Andrew Matthews	£2.50
☐	7497 0420 9	**I Don't Want To!**	Bel Mooney	£2.50
☐	7497 0833 6	**Melanie and the Night Animal**	Gillian Rubinstein	£2.50
☐	7497 0264 8	**Akimbo and the Elephants**	A McCall Smith	£2.50
☐	7497 0048 3	**Friends and Brothers**	Dick King-Smith	£2.50
☐	7497 0795 X	**Owl Who Was Afraid of the Dark**	Jill Tomlinson	£2.99

All these books are available at your bookshop or newsagent, or can be ordered direct from the publisher. Just tick the titles you want and fill in the form below.

Mandarin Paperbacks, Cash Sales Department, PO Box 11, Falmouth, Cornwall TR10 9EN.

Please send cheque or postal order, no currency, for purchase price quoted and allow the following for postage and packing:

UK including BFPO   £1.00 for the first book, 50p for the second and 30p for each additional book ordered to a maximum charge of £3.00.

Overseas including Eire   £2 for the first book, £1.00 for the second and 50p for each additional book thereafter.

NAME (Block letters) ....

ADDRESS ....

....

☐ I enclose my remittance for ....

☐ I wish to pay by Access/Visa Card Number

Expiry Date